"Mr. Belmont, Surely My Duties Are Ended for the Night?"

she asked curtly and started to turn from him, but his hands shot out and caught her shoulders.

"Not yet, Miss Lacey, not yet," he said with razor-edged softness. His grip tightened on her shoulders, pulling her toward him, his mouth settling on hers so suddenly that she had no time to react.

Christina's shocked cry was smothered by the hard, warm mouth pressing urgently on hers. His arms curled around her, tightening until she was trapped against his dizzying warmth and she could feel his heart thudding as violently as her own.

ASHLEY SUMMERS

lives in Spring, Texas, where she keeps a "ten-room house, a fat Schnauzer, a grouchy cat and occasionally a grandson." She has several writing projects under way, and the most important influence on her work is her "fantastic husband."

Dear Reader:

I'd like to take this opportunity to thank you for all your support and encouragement of Silhouette Romances.

Many of you write in regularly, telling us what you like best about Silhouette, which authors are your favorites. This is a tremendous help to us as we strive to publish the best contemporary romances possible.

All the romances from Silhouette Books are for you, so enjoy this book and the many stories to come. I hope you'll continue to share your thoughts with us, and invite you to write to us at the address below:

Karen Solem
Editor-in-Chief
Silhouette Books
P.O. Box 769
New York, N.Y. 10019

ASHLEY SUMMERS
Season of Enchantment

Silhouette *Romance*
Published by Silhouette Books New York
America's Publisher of Contemporary Romance

Other Silhouette Books by Ashley Summers

Fires of Memory

SILHOUETTE BOOKS, a Simon & Schuster Division of
GULF & WESTERN CORPORATION
1230 Avenue of the Americas, New York, N.Y. 10020

ISBN: 0-671-57197-4

First Silhouette Books printing January, 1983

10 9 8 7 6 5 4 3 2 1

All of the characters in this book are fictitious. Any resem-
blance to actual persons, living or dead, is purely coincidental.

Map by Ray Lundgren

Season of
Enchantment

Chapter One

Christina Lacey replaced the telephone with a rueful smile. Aunt Pauline seemed more annoyed than concerned with her niece's accident. But then, Aunt Pauline had a right to be annoyed, Christina wryly admitted. She had certainly made a fine mess of things. The dull throb of pain accompanying her involuntary sniffle was a persistent reminder of the situation she had brought about.

Swinging her shapely legs off the bed, she walked to the mirror and forced herself to look. Gingerly she explored the swollen blob that had once been a small pert nose. When the splinted bandage had been removed she had come as close to fainting as she likely ever would, but Dr. Maason had assured her that the reconstruction had gone well, and that she would again look like Christina Lacey—perhaps minutely altered, but the difference would be too slight to be noticeable.

At the moment, she looked nothing less than grotesque, she thought bitterly, wincing as she touched a particularly tender spot. "Happy birthday, Christina. Oh, good grief, *don't* start crying—you can't even blow your nose!" she admonished the woebegone face in the mirror. And when had she started talking to herself? But the oppressive silence of this room would provoke a wooden Indian to speech. It had never been quiet at home, always someone laughing or singing or raising Cain. . . .

Christina suddenly felt her loneliness as something so tangible she could almost touch it. Aunt Pauline had called to say the white frame house had been sold and its furnishings auctioned off. While Christina appreciated her uncle's kindness in handling the painful matter, the finality of it was still capable of twisting her heart. The small four-room house had been home from the day she was born.

Realizing she was indulging in self-pity, Christina gingerly wiped her face and took up the hairbrush as a means of counteracting the threat of more tears. Crying seldom accomplished anything, she told herself sternly.

The sound of a car door shutting with a decisive bang suspended her hairbrush in midair. She heard voices and then a laugh—and there was only one man in the world who laughed like that! Deep, husky laughter reeking of that infuriating male assurance. Putting down the brush, she shook back her long black hair and wiped the tangled lashes fringing her violet eyes. Excitement surged through her as the laugh came again. Christina flew to the window and peeked out.

A long black car nestled in the carport adjoining the bungalow. Daniel Belmont had returned.

Christina's heart pounded as she spied on him. His back turned, his tall form partially obscured by the jasmine vine that screened the redwood deck, Daniel stood chatting with the pretty blond who occupied the adjacent cottage. Christina shamelessly listened, for she was burning with curiosity about this attractive man. She could distinguish the woman's sultry laugh mingling with his amused voice, but the conversation was too low to make out words.

Since she could not eavesdrop, Christina settled for watching her benefactor. It had been Daniel Belmont who had smashed her nose. At the precise moment his big car had rammed the rear of her small Honda, she had been reaching for something on the floor, and the impact had hurled her face first into the unpadded dash. Besides the damage to her nose, the protruding metal edge of the lockbox she kept on the dash had slashed her scalp, and she had painfully wrenched one wrist.

The first few days following her accident were blurred in her memory. Daniel Belmont had located the plastic surgeon, guaranteed her shockingly expensive hospital bills, sent her flowers, and paid four visits to the hospital, usually in late evening and usually five minutes long. He had been crisp, impatient, and patently annoyed at the responsibility he had assumed, although once she remembered, or thought she remembered, him touching her bruised cheek with a fingertip and saying softly, "I'll bet there's a pretty face under all of this."

When she had been released as an outpatient, Daniel materialized like a magic genie. He had settled her bill, escorted her to his car, and driven her to this luxurious bungalow. When she had dared

9

protest, he wearily advised her to please shut up—he had enough on his mind without her adding to it.

She was too confused and intimidated by the forceful man to oppose him. But when she saw her Honda, now repaired and repainted as well, parked in the drive, Christina had again tried to refuse his excessive generosity. Daniel had dismissed it with an authoritative wave of hand; he was responsible for her accident and thus obligated to see that she was fully restored to health. Since she was low on funds, a fact he ascertained by simply asking her, she would stay in his cottage until Dr. Maason released her. The cottage came with a maid; all Christina had to do was rest and heal.

It was a direct order. Christina had the feeling he would lock her up in a private sanitarium and enforce it if she dared oppose his plan!

She rested. She walked on the beach. She explored Corpus Christi, finding it exotically warm and beautiful after the frigid temperatures of Cleveland. The majestic palms silhouetted against a blue blue sky, the banks of blossoming azaleas, the balmy air itself were exhilarating delight. But she had worked since she was fourteen years old, and this enforced idleness, along with the feeling of being totally useless as well as dependent upon a stranger's charity, gnawed at her pride.

But she was healing. The stitches had been removed from her scalp and her wrist was no longer sore. Only the swelling around her nose remained, but each day this subsided a little more, and the disfiguring bruises were pale yellow shadows on her creamy skin.

Although he had called several times, Christina had seen Daniel Belmont only once during the ten days she had resided in his cottage. He had come in the soft blue dusk of evening and joined her on the terrace, staying only a few minutes and leaving her feeling wistfully depressed. After inquiring about her health, he idly mentioned that he would be out of town for several days, and that was the extent of their conversation. The fact that he displayed no curiosity about her background nor seemed aware that she was a woman, piqued her femininity. She found herself waiting for his return impatiently.

Christina shrank back as he turned and headed for the cottage. Too late she remembered the faded jeans and old yellow sweat shirt she wore. His long legs took the steps two at a time and she barely had time to leap on the couch and assume a casual pose before he walked in the door.

Aggravated by this, she looked at him and said coldly, "You could have knocked, you know. I might have been indecent."

"I doubt very seriously that that would have disturbed me," Daniel pleasantly returned. "But I apologize. How are you feeling?"

"Much better, thank you," she said frostily. Daniel walked to the couch and stood towering over her imperiously. "Stand up. Let me look at you."

Her mouth tightening, Christina obstinately remained seated. He waited. Fuming, she got to her feet and stood with her head held in unconscious challenge. His long, tanned fingers gently grasped her chin as he turned her face from side to side, then checked her wrist and worked her fingers.

"You'd think you were buying a horse," she said sullenly. "Any minute now you'll examine my teeth!" His face was so close she could see the faint white scar on one cheek and the individual hairs of his sooty lashes. His clean male scent was faintly tinged with a spicy cologne she found very pleasing, and his fingers were caressingly warm on her skin. Shaken by her reaction to his impersonal touch, she snapped, "Are you about finished, Mr. Belmont?"

The full mouth twitched. "Um, I suppose so. Well, you seem all together—no pieces missing," he drawled, releasing her wrist. "I assume your nose will look better in time. May I sit down?"

"It's your cottage," she said with scant civility.

"So it is. I talked with Maason today—he says another two or three weeks and you should look presentable," he stated, sinking down in a chair. "I could use a drink—do you know how to fix a decent drink?"

"No, I don't."

Daniel heaved himself erect with a slanting glance for her sullen tone. "Take your hand down from your face," he said as he strode to the small, elegant bar tucked into an alcove off the kitchen. Guiltily, Christina obeyed, realizing this was a newly acquired habit, shielding her injury from inquisitive eyes.

"Tell me, Mr. Belmont, are you generally this obnoxious, or am I getting special treatment?" she sweetly inquired. "And do you always make yourself at home in another person's house?"

"I generally do as I please," he mildly returned. "And may I remind you this is my house?"

"And may I remind you that you loaned it to me? Thus I am, at the moment, mistress of this house." Christina regretted the words the instant they were out, but she could not restrain the antagonism this man evoked.

Daniel chuckled. "Touché," he said, raising his

glass in mocking salute. "Oh, I beg your pardon— may I fix you a drink, Miss Lacey?"

"No, thank you. I don't drink," she said quietly.

"Ah . . . nor smoke?"

"No."

The glinting green eyes roamed over her. "Nor indulge in any sinful pleasures of the flesh, hm, Miss Lacey?" he asked silkily.

"I'm not promiscuous, if that's your question," she coolly replied.

Daniel looked amused. "I certainly didn't mean to infer that." He took a long swallow and leaned back against the bar, his eyes on her face. "Happy birthday, Miss Christina Lacey," he murmured, raising his glass again.

"Oh! Why, thank you. How did you know it was my birthday?"

"Your driver's license." Giving every appearance of staying awhile, he settled more comfortably against the bar and continued, "It also listed your home as Cleveland, Ohio, but you told me you were from Harlingen—"

"I didn't say I was from Harlingen, I said I was *coming* from there," she corrected, wondering why this sudden interest.

"What were you doing in Harlingen?"

The question caught her off guard. Christina had hoped to avoid discussing painfully personal details. There seemed no way of explaining her presence in Texas without asking for pity, and the thought of pity from this man was exceedingly distasteful.

She clasped her hands in her lap and said as flatly as possible, "I was burying my mother."

"Your mother was from here?"

13

When Christina looked up, sea-green eyes were devoid of expression. Much relieved, she said steadily, "No, but my father is buried near there, and I thought she— I loved her very much and I wanted her to be near my father, so I brought her here, you see," she ended in a little rush.

The sleek dark head lowered to study the amber liquid in his glass. "My condolences, Miss Lacey," he said quietly.

"Thank you, but they're not necessary. My mother was in pain for months before she died and her death was . . . was a joyous relief to me," Christina said, hoping he would drop the subject.

"I see. One thing I don't understand. You drove here from Ohio?"

"No, I flew down."

"But you were driving a car when we regrettably became acquainted," he observed.

"Regrettably is right," she muttered, and instantly felt ashamed. Glancing at the quietly composed face, Christina responded more sensibly. "My father's cousin has a used-car lot in Harlingen. The Honda was pretty beat up, so he offered it to me for little more than the cost of my air fare home. I was in no great rush to return, so . . ." She trailed off.

The silence stretched out as he topped off his drink and added more ice cubes. Christina covertly studied his arrogant profile. The set of his mouth and that determined jaw bespoke a will that would not be crossed, she thought with a little shiver. A curious thrill raced through her as the emerald eyes set on her face again. It was fascinating how swiftly they changed color—everything from the crispness of new leaves to this deep jewellike hue.

"So. What are you going to do, go back to Ohio?" he asked.

"I haven't decided yet. I—I've sort of fallen in love with Corpus. It's a lovely city. And there's nothing back home. Just some relatives, but we—my mother and I—were never really close to them. And Dave is—"

"Dave?" he prompted as she faltered.

"My—a man I knew," she said lamely.

"Ah, a lost lover," he said with a sardonic grin. "Run out on you, did he?"

"That's none of your business!" Christina said hotly.

"You're absolutely right. Nor am I particularly interested." Daniel swung across the room and stood studying her. "Do you have any money at all?"

The question was so sharp she blinked. "I can manage."

"That's debatable, but it isn't what I asked."

"That isn't any of your business either, Mr. Belmont."

"I'm making it my business," he stated arrogantly, sitting down again.

"Tell me, are you usually this concerned with the women you run down?" she jibed.

"I don't usually run down women. And I hate having smashed-up little girls on my conscience. *Do* you have any plans, or are you just drifting along hoping someone will come to the rescue?"

Christina felt her cheeks flaming. Her plans were too nebulous to hurl back at him. "I told you my plans are still up in the air," she said stiffly.

Daniel got up and began pacing the floor. From

under her lashes Christina watched his lean, handsome figure, noting the muscular arm that raised above his head as he absently massaged one shoulder. He reminded her of a sleek panther with that aura of leashed power and the feline grace of his movements. The soft red shirt he wore was superb contrast to his dark hair and bronzed skin, and his dark gray slacks were expertly tailored to his strong masculine lines.

Resentful of the way his looks distracted her, Christina was torn between wishing he would go and hoping he would stay. When he turned to face her again, his eyes caught on the curves of her breasts. Idly he appraised her snug-fitting jeans before taking another turn around the room. She knew remarkably little about the man other than facts gleaned from newspaper gossip. He was an eminently eligible bachelor, a native of Texas, and one of Corpus Christi's most prominent citizens, and he liked beautiful women.

Judging from the number of times she had been photographed on his arm, his favorite was Lisa Manning, "stunningly beautiful socialite."

Discomfited by his silence, Christina blurted, "Mr. Belmont, do you ordinarily live in this cottage?"

"Of course not. I have a condominium—the cottage is for pleasure."

"What kind of pleasure?" she asked unthinkingly.

"All kinds," he absently replied. Christina flushed. He glanced at her, his amused green eyes taking note of her discomfort. And enjoying it, she thought hotly. "Miss Lacey, I have a dinner engagement this evening. Now, do you have any money?"

"A little—"

"And do you have any plans beyond occupying my cottage for the rest of your life?" he asked sourly.

"I'll be out of here as soon as possible—you can be sure of that."

"Oh, I'm sure of that," Daniel replied with a sigh. She was curled up on the couch with her little bare feet tucked under her bottom and her curly black hair tumbling around the small, damaged face, and the sight of her was somehow unsettling.

At least, she observed in surprise, he looked at her unhappily, with something very near irritated tenderness, before turning back to the window. She had caught that peculiar expression in his eyes several times while she was in the hospital, but she assumed it a natural reaction to her pathetic appearance. However, she didn't think she looked pathetic now—a little ugly, she conceded, but hardly pathetic. Then why the look?

Christina blushed clear to the roots of her hair as she suddenly comprehended the reason. He simply wanted her out of his house and his hair, and he was seeking a graceful exit.

"Mr. Belmont, I've become much stronger this past week—quite up to taking care of myself," she said earnestly. "I'm nearly well—"

"You're well when the doctor says you're well," he said so sharply she gave no argument. She didn't need his permission to leave!

"I'm not a man given to whimsy," he said reflectively. One hand prowled through his hair and settled on the back of his neck. "In fact, I've never done a foolish thing in my life that I can recall," he added, sounding faintly perplexed.

Since the remark seemed directed at himself, Christina remained silent. "How good are your clerical skills?" he asked abruptly.

"Excellent. Five years' experience."

"In what capacity?"

"Private secretary for my—in a small real estate firm. I also handled all the bookkeeping."

"How do you react to pressure—meeting deadlines, getting yelled at for the smallest infraction?" he rapped out.

"I function exceedingly well under pressure, and getting yelled at comes with the territory." A tiny smile tilted her lips. "However, I have also been known to yell back when the occasion warrants."

The other questions were rapid-fire, but this one came slowly. "Have you seriously considered staying in Texas?"

"Yes, I've thought about it. But I haven't come to any firm decision. My employer was very understanding about—about everything, and my job's still available. Or was the last time I heard. If not, I can easily find another one," she ended firmly, feeling inexpressibly weary at the thought of taking up her life again. No one needed her now—no one waited eagerly at day's end for her return. . . .

Realizing he had turned to face her again, she lowered her head and sought composure. It was foreign to her nature to have no clear-cut goals or direction, and she had an urgent desire to explain this, to make him see she was not always this vague, indecisive creature. She looked up and gave him a soft, reassuring smile to make up for her long silence.

Daniel frowned as he regarded her. His hair had been tousled by his restless hand and it softened his somewhat formidable mien. The dark brows knit into a line at her spontaneous little laugh. He attempted sternness, but his eyes suddenly crinkled in a responsive grin.

He snapped it off. Christina uncurled her legs and sat with hands demurely folded, enjoying her glimpse of a likable man concealed in that stern mask.

"All right now, I'm in a hurry, so I'll tell you my idea," said Daniel severely. "You can remain here until you become a little less unsightly, after which time you will report to my office at . . ." He took out his wallet and extended a business card. "At this address. You *can* take dictation, can't you?" he testily inquired, glancing at her astonished eyes as he replaced his wallet.

Christina sought words, but her head was spinning, and all that came out of her at first was a startled "Oh!" Then, feeling foolishly defiant, she added, "Can't everyone?"

Daniel sighed deeply. "No, not everyone. However, your job will include more personal duties . . ."

When Christina jumped to her feet in surprise, he threw back his head and laughed. "Miss Lacey, believe me, I have no designs on you—you're not my type of woman," he murmured with a diffident glance down her body. Ignoring her gasp, he continued. "By personal duties I meant that you will accompany me on trips, in the capacity of personal secretary—"

Abashed at her presumption, Christina interrupted, "I don't understand—don't you already have a personal secretary?"

"Yes I do, but she rather reminds me of a charmingly plump otter, and her conversation is not too scintillating," he drawled. "I don't particularly enjoy her company . . ." His eyes gleamed behind thick black lashes. "I'm not too sure I'll enjoy yours, but that's of little consequence—if I don't, you're fired. It's as simple as that."

Christina stared her confusion. "I still don't understand—exactly what is the job?"

He sighed and raked a hand through his hair. "I'll try to explain," he said patiently. "I travel, Miss Lacey. My work is exceedingly demanding and I need someone to do things like keep track of my schedule, take notes at meetings, fix me a drink, pour my coffee, see that my plane is ready when I am, sit on that plane and take dictation or talk to me or whatever. Are you beginning to understand yet?"

Daniel didn't wait for a reply. "I have a personal *office* secretary. I want a personal Daniel Belmont secretary—someone utterly devoted to me, subject to my whims—a personal attendant, you might say." He grinned. "A luxury, I admit, but one I can afford. And there are times when I desperately need it. Do you understand?"

"I guess so," she said so doubtfully he hid a smile. "Who did all this before me?"

"Another young lady."

"And what happened to that other young lady?"

A sardonic note entered his voice. "Unfortunately she developed delusions of grandeur. The fringe benefits that go with the job do not include control of my life or becoming my wife."

Christina's head snapped up. "Fringe benefits? Just precisely what are those fringe benefits, Mr. Belmont?" she asked coolly.

"What do you think they are, Miss Lacey?" he baited.

"Are you saying there's more to the job than just attending meetings and taking dictation and—and pouring your coffee?"

"That, of course, is up to you. If you're so inclined—well, we'll see," he said carelessly. "Right now you're not too appetizing, but perhaps you'll improve."

Christina went white with anger. "You actually think I'd want to—to—" she sputtered furiously. The arrogance of the man!

Daniel laughed aloud. "My, you do blaze up quickly . . . interesting," he murmured.

"If you think you can *demand*—" she began heatedly.

"I never demand anything from a woman. But then, I don't have to."

Catching the undercurrent of amusement in his voice, Christina clenched her hands. "Forgive me for doubting your word, Mr. Belmont, but I frankly see nothing that would lead me to believe you are completely irresistible to women," she said with scathing scorn.

An eyebrow arched. "Why, Miss Lacey, you wound me. May I point out it was you who jumped to conclusions? I said nothing about a personal relationship. I simply want someone to take as much off my shoulders as possible. As for my lack of appeal, perhaps we shall test your immunity, but it will have to be at a later date—I really am pressed for time."

The sarcasm in his voice stung Christina to a furious retort. "Mr. Belmont, I don't think I have *ever* met a more arrogant, conceited, high-handed male!"

"Miss Lacey, your opinion of me is neither important nor desired. And considering the circumstances, I doubt whether it's even wise," he mocked.

Christina wilted under the hard truth of this. "I'm sorry. I didn't mean . . ." She tipped her chin. "All right, I apologize. And I am grateful for your kindness—"

"I should certainly hope so."

"Well, you're the one who ran into me! It's your fault I have this horrible face and got s-stuck in this town—"

He sighed. "Please, spare me the tears? I detest a female's penchant for bursting into tears at the slightest provocation."

"Slightest provocation?"

Daniel winced at the outraged shriek. "And one more thing. You'll need some clothes—stylish, expensive, attractive clothes. I don't enjoy dowdy kittens any more than I enjoy charming otters."

"I loathe being called a kitten."

Daniel graciously overlooked her remark. "A clothing allowance is one of the fringe benefits of the job. My secretary will open accounts at suitable shops—oh, when you report to her, use the title of . . . personal assistant. Good night, Miss Lacey."

"You come back here, damn it!" Christina exploded as he strode toward the door.

Daniel paused with his hand on the knob. "I also dislike profanity," he reproved. "Surely you don't still have questions?"

Feeling utterly unhinged, Christina sat back down on the couch and regarded his face. His features were too irregular to be called handsome in the strictest sense of the word, yet he was compellingly handsome. The pulse throbbing at the base of her throat testified to that. Meeting his dispassionate gaze, Christina felt chastened. She had reacted to his generosity like a sullen child, she ruefully admitted to herself.

She spread her hands in a little gesture of apology. "Yes. I have one question, Mr. Belmont. Why are you doing this for me?" she asked quietly, her violet eyes wide and steady on his face.

A ghost of a smile touched his mouth as he rumpled his hair again. "To be truthful, I don't know. Perhaps it's because I still feel obligated . . . or maybe it's because you are obviously about as responsible as a two-year-old let loose to play on the street. Or maybe—" He grinned. "Or maybe I have a weakness for stray kittens. I'll see you in my office. Good night, Miss Lacey."

Control, Christina, control, she admonished herself, feeling a stinging itch to belt the man. Rising to her feet, she shook back her hair and faced him with imperious pride. "No, you won't see me in your office. You've done enough already. I'm quite satisfied that your so-called debt is paid in full, and anything else would be charity. And I don't want your charity, Mr. Belmont. So thanks, but no thanks."

The cynical green eyes moved over her in lingering appraisal. "Believe me, it won't be charity—you'll earn every cent of that salary. But who knows? You might even enjoy it. I'll see you in three weeks, Miss Lacey." The dark head inclined in an insolent farewell before he strode out the door.

Christina sank limply on the couch, her mind racing at dizzying speed. She had never heard of the kind of job he offered. A personal secretary, yes, but a personal *attendant*? He could afford such luxury, he said, and he had a plane at his disposal.

He was, she guessed, in his early thirties, yet his confident manner was that of a much older man. How had he acquired it so young? She felt positively green-apple raw in his presence!

Why had he offered her what looked at face value to be a splendid opportunity? Feeling obligated for her recovery was creditable, but stretching it to include responsibility for her future welfare simply stretched it too thin. Was he attracted to her? She snorted at the thought—what was there to attract him? In truth, she looked more comical than tragic, and he had never seen her any other way.

Temporarily shelving this puzzle, it dawned on her that she had forgotten to ask the nature of his business. Picking up the business card, she studied it in the last rays of sunlight, smiling softly at the boldness of his name. "Daniel Belmont . . . Belmont Enterprises," she read aloud. It had a fine ring to it, but it didn't explain anything.

Her eyes deepened as she thought of entire days spent in that exciting presence. Despite the fact that she had been struck several times with an urge to slap that handsome face, she had felt a tingling current of excitement the entire time he was in the room. Startled by this, she tried to recall how it had been with Dave. A soft, warm sensation, like being held and cuddled when you've fallen and skinned your knee, she thought wryly. Dave had never been more than mildly passionate about anything, including her. But Daniel Belmont would be intensely passionate, particularly with his women. . . .

She shivered. She had never known a man's passion, nor been forced to combat her own. She didn't even know if she was capable of passion. The golden ideal of marriage and home and children had always seemed far more important than the intimacy of love.

Her mouth set as she considered her two-year relationship with the quiet, soft-spoken Dave Townsend. He was sixteen years older and infinitely more experienced, and in retrospect it was easy to see what he offered—a warm, affectionate friendship. The depths of her self-deception amazed her. For a twenty-three-year-old woman who was presumably intelligent and perceptive, she had behaved like a silly little fool. . . .

Christina was rather surprised to find herself striding along the moonlit beach. Jamming her hands into her pockets, she trudged along with head lowered to the night wind. The job Daniel dangled before her was maddeningly tempting. For a brief moment she found herself speculating on her unaccountable reaction to the man, but that was neither here nor there.

The clothing allowance disturbed her. It seemed demeaning to have her employer—and particularly *this* employer—pay for her attire. However, a sensible person faced facts, she grimly reminded herself; deduct the expense of office wear, and the salary he offered became a princely sum.

And she was deeply in debt. Her mother's medical expenses had far exceeded their small insurance policy. While the proceeds from the sale of their home would cover most of them, there was still the matter of a personal loan for funeral expenses and air fare to Texas and a thousand other details that cropped up like weeds after a summer rain. Her uncle would not press her for the money, but he and Pauline were people of modest means, and she felt obligated to repay them.

Idly she leaned against a rough gray pylon and

watched the moon. If she took Daniel Belmont's astonishing offer, it would not be a serene relationship. She was not known for meekness, and he certainly displayed no signs of a tolerant nature. They were like flint and stone, she mused; the two could not come together without sparks!

Oddly enough, the prospect did not dismay her. She felt alive and eager again, and everything had a sparkling clarity, as if she had walked out of a fog of confusion into the clean morning light. Working with Daniel would be a constant challenge. He would be demanding and likely bad tempered, and she had no doubt he would exact full value from every cent of her salary. With her skills she would have no difficulty finding an easier, possibly more pleasant position, but she *wanted* the challenge of matching herself against whatever he required of her. Proving that she was adequate to the task seemed infinitely desirable.

Ignoring the image of his lean, hawkish face, she stared across the wide silver path of the moon. "I will be Daniel Belmont's secretary," she said testingly. Her voice grew stronger. "I will earn that salary —I will give full value for every penny! And someday . . ."

Her flaring excitement died. Someday was too far away. It was enough right now to cope with the decision to take Daniel Belmont's job.

Chapter Two

Exactly three weeks and a Monday later, Christina gave her appearance a final check before reporting for work. Until she was actively on the job, she did not feel it proper to use the clothing allowance and was making do with her own wardrobe.

Critical examination of her navy linen coat dress revealed nothing to detract from the crucially important image of chic young career woman. Leaning closer, she peered at her face. The feature known as a pug nose was now subtly redefined into a pert tilt of flared nostrils, and her violet eyes glowed with excited apprehension. She was not beautiful, nor could she ever hope to be, but she was attractive. At least, *she* thought so.

Noting the time, Christina slipped on navy blue pumps, gave her neatly coiled chignon a pat, and hastened down the stairs. She had moved from Daniel's cottage a week ago and taken a furnished room with kitchen privileges at Tate's Boarding House, an ancient frame dwelling that fronted on an alley and backed up to a large warehouse. The noise was constant but the rent was cheap, and at the moment Christina valued the low rent above all else. By keeping her living expenses to a minimum she could begin to pay back her debts.

Wheeling into the stream of traffic, she drove with half a mind to the task. The thought of seeing Daniel again left her oddly breathless and uneasy. He had come once more to the beach house, a five-minute visit that naturally caught her windblown and blue-jeaned on the beach. He examined her nose, inquired as to her health, said he would see her in a week, and walked off with a jaunty wave of his hand.

Once again he had turned her into a stammering schoolgirl, Christina admitted. But no more! She would be cool and efficient, a poised young woman with a confidence Daniel Belmont couldn't put a dent in. And above all else she would not be intimidated by a dreadfully intimidating man.

The Belmont Tower was a pillar of gold-tinted glass and concrete with a parking deck for employees. Christina circled for several minutes before she found a spot for her Honda. She took the elevator to the twelfth floor and followed the blue carpet to the door of a large reception room. Here she stopped to gather composure and firmly repeat all the things she absolutely would not do.

She need not have bothered. Mr. Belmont was out of town for the entire week. Furthermore, when she presented herself to Mrs. Coyle, the guardian of the inner sanctum, the woman's practiced smile slipped a notch; not only did Christina not have a desk, but

Mrs. Coyle, executive secretary to Daniel Belmont, hadn't the faintest idea that she was joining the firm.

Flushed with embarrassment, Christina glanced around the attractive room, which contained, besides the surprised Mrs. Coyle, a glassed cubicle off to one side where two smartly dressed young women pecked at typewriters. It was a pleasant enough atmosphere in which to work—if one didn't feel like a rank imposter!

She stood quietly aside while Mrs. Coyle called Personnel and discretely verified her claim. Why hadn't Daniel mentioned her joining the firm? Christina wondered uneasily. He himself had suggested she go to the personnel office and file the necessary forms, which she had done, and she thus assumed she would be, if not welcome, at least expected. Maybe it was her fault for waiting so long. She had only done so Friday afternoon. Obviously Personnel hadn't gotten around to notifying Mrs. Coyle. Feeling shorn of a great deal of her assurance, Christina tried not to fidget during the embarrassing call.

Evidently it was satisfactory; maintaining her impassive mien, Mrs. Coyle escorted her into Daniel's private office. It was starkly handsome, much like the man himself, Christina thought, touching the massive desk that dominated the room. The only personal item was a tiny sculpture of a deer carved from deep red wood. She picked it up and stroked the satiny texture. Replacing it in the exact same spot, she tried his chair but felt such an upstart intruder she settled for the russet leather couch that fronted the window.

Mrs. Coyle soon returned with the two office girls, who were introduced as Judy and Diana and quickly dismissed. The smartly dressed woman did remind Christina of a charmingly plump otter. Repressing a nervous giggle, she listened with grave attention as Mrs. Coyle listed the shops she thought appropriate. Since she need only call and reopen the accounts, she suggested Christina attend to her wardrobe before anything else.

A slanted glance down Christina's inexpensive frock reinforced the suggestion. Christina didn't mind. This seemed a remarkably lovely way to spend her first day on the job! She stopped by Personnel to obtain a plastic-coated card proclaiming her new position and headed for the shopping center.

The next few days passed slowly. When she wasn't acting in the capacity of glorified office boy, Christina spent her time familiarizing herself with the building and Daniel's business. His interests were bewilderingly diverse and seemingly in a constant state of flux. Mrs. Coyle indulgently described him as a workaholic. This did not strike Christina as too admirable a thing to be, but apparently in Texas it was.

Mrs. Coyle's esteem was laced with maternal affection; they had been together six years now, and she thought Daniel a most considerate boss. Christina thought sourly that she must know a different Daniel Belmont. However, such judgment could not be faulted; while it was perfectly normal for the office girls to worship at his feet, Mrs. Coyle was levelheaded enough to evaluate anyone's character, including Christina's.

She was still uncomfortable that Daniel had bought the clothes she now wore, but when she delicately probed the issue, Mrs. Coyle's surprise provoked a guilty flush. "It's just that I feel rather odd, having him buy my clothes—"

"Mr. Belmont doesn't buy them, Belmont Enterprises does," Mrs. Coyle crisply corrected. "It's standard procedure, Miss Lacey. Mr. Belmont realizes this particular position requires an extensive wardrobe that's usually beyond the average working woman's means. Thus he provides a clothing allowance as a basic part of your salary."

"Do other companies practice this policy?" Christina dared.

A frosty note entered Mrs. Coyle's voice. "I'm sure I don't know about other companies. I work for Mr. Belmont. And so do you, Miss Lacey."

Christina got the distinct impression that to question Mr. Belmont's ethics—or anything else—was a crime just short of treason.

Relenting, Mrs. Coyle took a file from his cabinet and handed it to Christina. "Perhaps this might help you. It's a profile on Mr. Belmont done two years ago by the *Texas Businessman's Monthly*," she said impressively, then quietly left the room.

Looking impressed wasn't too difficult, Christina thought wryly. Daniel's business acumen was obvious even to her. He had begun Belmont Enterprises with the small construction company inherited from his father. Discovering that several concerns owed the firm substantial sums but were unable to pay upon demand, he had taken an ownership position in those companies and within a year found himself owner or partial owner of a hotel, a textile plant, and a housing development.

According to the reporter, Daniel had an ingrained knack for being able to cut to the heart of a business problem and was ruthless in doing what was required to make these various companies profitable.

Christina frowned. Thinking of Daniel in terms of *ruthless* did not set too well. A little surprised at her feeling of loyalty, she read on. He had further developed his business by accepting construction contracts and taking his fee in stock. Belmont Enterprises formed the corporate parent for his wide-ranging interests, which included Belmont Construction, Westgate Textiles, Eastern Hotels, Belmont Real Estate, and Pacific Shipping.

Wishing it had included a few personal details on the man himself, Christina set aside the report and considered her job in a new light. All these activities kept him traveling a great deal, and an administrative assistant who could travel with him and support his efforts looked more like a necessity than a luxury. Her job was neither frivolous nor subject to scorn; she would be a vital part of Belmont Enterprises.

Glowing with new determination, Christina replaced the file and took out several others for an in-depth study. She would be the best assistant Daniel ever had!

If being a valid part of his firm eased her mind, it was nonetheless an interminably long week. Friday evening Christina was just preparing to leave when Daniel suddenly materialized. She was in his office at the time. Her heart pounding with conflicting emotions, she jumped to her feet and swiftly smoothed her dress and hair.

Daniel stepped inside the door and abruptly stopped. There was startled surprise in his eyes and a flaring gleam of something else she could not fathom. The moment spun out, taut and ringingly tense.

Christina had the sensation of hanging suspended in those emerald depths as he scrutinized every inch of her, from the top of her head to the tips of her classic brown pumps.

Christina felt a distinct shock when his gaze finally tangled with hers. She heard the release of her breath, and his, and then the timeless moment shattered with his sardonic quirk of eyebrow.

"Good evening, Miss Lacey. I'm glad to see you're fully recovered. You look very well. By the way, this is *my* office," he lightly stressed.

Stung, Christina retorted, "Good evening, Mr. Belmont—and what was I supposed to do, sit in a corner? I have no desk of my own."

A smile touched his mouth. "I see. Well, we'll have to rectify that—"

"And you didn't even bother telling Mrs. Coyle that you had a new assistant. Did it slip your mind?" she rushed on.

"At times trivial details do slip my mind, I admit, but I'm a busy man, Miss Lacey. However, in this case may I remind you that you did not do me the courtesy of formally accepting the job? I had no idea whether or not you'd show up," he lazily protested. His face was turned from her as he spoke, yet Christina sensed a grin on that handsome mouth.

"The last time I checked with Personnel, you weren't listed," he added.

"Well, I didn't decide until the last minute," she said lamely. His look was ample response. Suddenly aware that he was baiting her, Christina lifted her chin. "However, I did come in last Friday and fill out the forms as you suggested, and I have now been here a week—as you very well know," she ended a trifle warmly.

He took his time answering her charge. "Umm. Well, Mrs. Coyle assures me that you used the week constructively. I assume you now consider yourself capable of handling the job . . ." A sudden grin matched the silky note entering his voice as his gaze flickered over her again. "And me?"

Uncertain of his exact meaning, Christina coolly replied, "I think it's within my capabilities, yes."

Daniel turned his back. "It should prove interesting finding out, at any rate," he remarked.

Christina saw that she had been mistaken. It was not the desk that dominated the room; it was the man who sat down behind it who commanded all her attention. He wore a light gray suit, tailored with an attractive Western flair, casually elegant, yet somehow austere. His hair sprung back from a sharp widow's peak off center of his forehead, leaving a lock eternally atilt over one dark eyebrow. Studying his face, she realized with an absurd little shock that this was a dangerously good-looking man, one who knew to the smallest degree just what effect he had on a woman. And would use it if it suited his purpose, she thought uneasily.

Contrarily, when he glanced up at her impatient movement, Christina was shaken by his impersonal gaze. She wore a beige dress, and for a wild moment she wondered if she had faded into the honey-hued paneling that covered his walls.

Daniel stood up, stuffed several files into his briefcase, and walked past her. The sleek head inclined in courteous recognition. "I hope you enjoy your weekend, Miss Lacey. I'll see you Monday morning."

"Thank you, Mr. Belmont. Monday morning," she echoed. Watching him swing back through the reception room, Christina clenched her fists. She had been summarily dismissed, left feeling disappointed and obscurely insulted and without a valid reason for either emotion.

Just as he reached the door, a tall, slender woman with red gold hair came dashing in. Christina caught only a brief glimpse of her face, but she saw the quick kiss as Daniel caught and steadied the woman, and the arm curving possessively around her shoulders as they walked out the door.

She hurried to Mrs. Coyle's desk. "Who was that, Mrs. Coyle?"

Mrs. Coyle's eyebrows arched. "I imagine it's been ages since anyone in Corpus asked that question about Lisa Manning," she laughed.

"Are they . . . is he going to marry her?"

"She thinks so," Mrs. Coyle said, dry as dust.

Monday morning Christina was pleasantly surprised to find a parking slot bearing her name and even more pleased when the guard tipped his hat and greeted her by name. As she walked into the reception room, Mrs. Coyle looked up with a subtly different smile.

"He wants you to go right in," she said as though conferring an honor. Both office girls called cheery greetings. What had altered her status? Christina wondered. She tapped lightly, then entered at Daniel's terse command. With a glance at her garnet jersey dress, he nodded and handed her a sheet of paper.

"This is our schedule for the week. From now on you will receive one every Friday so you will be prepared. Prepared means having a bag packed and ready to go on schedule. I prefer your hair up during business hours," he said, looking pointedly at the softly curling mass framing her face. "Look this over, go home, pack a bag, and meet me here in forty minutes."

"Yes, sir," Christina said crisply. Her eyes widened as he uncoiled from his chair and stood in front of her. Daniel took a strand of her hair and rubbed it between his fingers the way a man rubs silk. His flat green gaze lingering on her mouth, he reminded, "Forty minutes, Miss Lacey," then sat down again, leaving her standing there looking at the top of his head. She was dismissed.

Thirty-eight minutes later she was back at the office and they left immediately for the airport. Half running to keep up with his long strides, Christina approached the small blue and silver plane warily. Daniel introduced her to the pilot, a short, cherub-faced man who looked far too young to be piloting a plane. She managed to fasten her seatbelt, but the last person to use it must have been a two-hundred-pound man, and she fumbled with it until he leaned over and did it for her.

"Do you get airsick?" he asked.

"No, I don't," she said, hoping it was true. She'd never flown in such a small plane—who knew how she'd react! She hoped he would miss her apprehension, but as the Navaho soared into the air, it made a stomach-lurching dip and her swift intake of breath was dismayingly audible.

"Miss Lacey, you have flown before?"

"Certainly. But not in small planes," she confessed.

"Heaven have mercy," muttered Daniel. He pulled out a table from the wall and unfolded it between them. Minutes later, he was absorbed in his work.

Christina sat quietly enjoying the view from her window, but eventually it palled. She fidgeted. Daniel looked up with a resigned, "Is anything wrong, Miss Lacey?"

Flushing at the annoyance in his voice, she said, "No, I—well, I thought you wanted scintillating conversation."

"Sometimes I do, sometimes I don't. Right now I don't." He reached behind him and withdrew a silver thermos and two cups emblazoned with the Belmont crest. "I drink a lot of coffee. I take it black, with two sugars, and I detest lukewarm coffee. See to it that my cup is kept filled and hot."

"That's it? Keeping your coffee cup filled and hot?"

His gaze trailed lazily over her bodice. "For now, yes."

"Mr. Belmont," Christina began indignantly.

Daniel burst out laughing. "Miss Lacey, if you will just let me finish this report, I promise we'll discuss your other duties. . . . My coffee?" he prompted.

Adding the final touches to her hair, Christina glanced at her watch. She was dressed and ready to go, but Daniel hadn't summoned her yet. Topping off her teacup, she sat down in a comfortable chair and leisurely sipped.

Another hotel room, another city. Raleigh this time. These past three weeks must surely rate as the most exhilarating, exhausting, utterly mad of her life, she thought wryly. She had run out of names for Daniel Belmont ages ago, but one thing she had to admit—he wasn't even remotely interested in anything beyond her professional skills.

Even his personal remarks pertained to business; she must at all times be immaculately groomed and her attire was subject to his approval or, in a few instances, his disapproval. He expected instant obedience to his orders and incompetence was inexcusable once she was familiar with her duties.

He permitted no profanity in her presence. When one gentleman saw fit to preface his remarks with a coarse expletive, Daniel mildly rebuked, "Gentlemen, please remember that Miss Lacey is here and that she is a lady."

Daniel himself was indefatigable. He conducted business in a brisk, no-nonsense manner, and she had already become aware that he was scrupulously honest in his dealings. She was awed by the man. That imperturbable mask was totally unruffled by people, events, or the terrifying storm they'd flown through last night. He had worked right through it and even managed to have his coffee.

She thought him an amazing man. Also a daunting one. During one meeting she had studied with increasing unease the portly man who represented the company Daniel wished to acquire. Christina debated with herself for agonizing minutes; Daniel might well resent interference and she wasn't sure she wished to risk a reprimand. But at last a sense of loyalty to her employer prevailed. When she managed to catch his eye, she made an almost imperceptible signal toward the door.

A fleeting frown had crossed his face before he suggested a short break. They went into the adjoining room. Closing the door behind him, Daniel irritably inquired, "All right. What is it, Miss Lacey?"

Her words had tumbled over each other in her eagerness to impress him. "Mr. Belmont, there's something wrong. That man—Mr. Powers? He's concealing something. Oh, I know he's doing a good job of it, but there's something he doesn't want to come out in this meeting."

"On what do you base your accusation?"

"Dave was a psychiatrist—he taught me how to read body language. It's very difficult to conceal inner tension, and Mr. Powers is a very tense man—much more so than just the sale of his company warrants," she stated.

Daniel studied her for a moment. "You're quite certain of this?"

"Certain enough to risk telling you," she said with a wry smile.

"I see. Thank you, Miss Lacey." Turning sharply, Daniel walked back into the meeting. Christina had listened with a kind of joyous disbelief as he courteously postponed it for a later date. A few days later her astute perception was given heed in a crisp, "Miss Lacey, I thank you for alerting me to Powers. It seems the company he represents will shortly be involved in an antitrust suit, subject to potential damages that could amount to millions of dollars."

No more was said, but after that Daniel took to casually asking her opinion—her *impressions,* really —on each and every meeting. That he valued her opinions at all pleased her all out of proportion, and she had an uneasy suspicion that her pleasure stemmed from something deeper than mere accomplishment. Even when she was so furious she could crown him with her typewriter, a secret part of her was vividly aware of that long, lean-muscled frame. . . .

The telephone's ringing command jarred her back to the present. Your master's voice, Christina, she thought, smiling at his brusque greeting. Regardless of how curt or impatient, his voice was to her ear as velvet is to caressing fingers.

She was to meet him downstairs in ten minutes, and since they were touring a construction site, he suggested slacks and sensible shoes. "You do have slacks?" He paused to check. She admitted she did not. Daniel sighed, ill-resigned to wait while she went downstairs and bought some.

"And thank you for starting my day off with a bang, Mr. Belmont," muttered Christina—after she'd hung up, of course. Rub velvet the wrong way, she smartingly reminded herself, and it felt much like sandpaper.

Despite this inauspicious beginning, it was a curiously bright, lovely day for Christina. After they left the plant site, Daniel treated her to lunch, a long, leisurely repast in the most charming seaside café imaginable.

"What would you like?" he inquired.

"Whatever you recommend," she replied recklessly. "I like all kinds of seafood!"

"Then we'll have oysters—"

"Except for oysters."

Grinning at her wrinkle of nose, Daniel ordered shrimp cocktails for two, broiled flounder for her, and three dozen oysters for himself. The shrimp was accompanied by a tangy hot sauce and the flounder, caught that morning, the waitress confided, was delicious. Watching Daniel apply himself to the oysters arrested Christina's attention in spite of her ravenous appetite. Accustomed to oysters on the half shell neatly laid out on a platter, she was fascinated by the lumpy gray chunks clustered around coral, each barely opened, requiring dexterity and what seemed to her an exceedingly avid desire to extract the succulent morsels.

Crispy fried potatoes, chunks of hot garlic bread, and a dish of crunchy relishes accompanied their meal. After polishing this off, Daniel independently decided they had room for dessert, and Christina groaned at the slabs of deep-dish apple pie topped with wedges of mellow cheddar carved from an enormous wheel that sat on the counter. Thick mugs of coffee washed it down. As if they had all the time in the world, Daniel ordered refills, and they sat back in relaxed comfort, chatting so easily she was totally unconscious of time's passage.

This was a new and fascinating Daniel Belmont, one who chivied her distaste for raw oysters and engaged her in a merry discussion of the mythical attributes given this particular seafood. She had not known he possessed such a sparkling wit, nor a flair for stating the absurd so gravely, she was torn between believing him and knowing perfectly well he was putting her on.

When they resumed the drive, Daniel turned down a narrow road that ran between a stretch of absolutely fabulous beaches. As soon as he stopped, Christina plunged from the car with all the guileless zest of a child. She had never seen such scenery—wild, harshly serene, with the pounding Atlantic on one side of enormous sand dunes and placid little canals on the other.

Brightly painted sailboats skimmed the sparkling

waters, and the wind filling their sails whipped her hair to glorious abandon. "Like it?" Daniel asked softly from behind her. She turned to him, her shining eyes giving him all the answer he needed.

"Oh, yes!" she exclaimed softly, a profound understatement. This stolen time with him was curiously close to creating a wild, singing rapture in her heart. He had taken off his tie and jacket, and as Christina was sure any woman would agree, a laughing, teasing Daniel Belmont with tousled hair and rolled-up shirt-sleeves equaled a state perilously near enchantment.

Gesturing to the sailboats, she said, "It looks like marvelous fun. Have you ever done it?"

"Certainly I have," Daniel said. "I'm an expert at it, too."

Glowing blue eyes raised to his at this statement. She laughed, her voice droll. "Of course."

His eyes crinkled. "Don't be impertinent, Miss Lacey," he said with mock severity.

She found her fingers loosely linked with his as they climbed the sand dunes. They paused on top for a panoramic view of the sea and the jewellike islands in the distance. The gusty wind flattened her shirt against her ripe breasts and tossed her hair around her shoulders. Knowing he was watching her, Christina stood proudly erect, her head tipped back in exciting awareness of her femininity. When she glanced at him, there was more than just laughter in his dark green eyes.

The pounding waves and wind made conversation impossible. "It's glorious!" she shouted in defiance of this.

The dark head dipped to hers. "Come along, Miss Lacey—before you take wing!" he laughed.

As they started back down, the crumbly dune gave way under her feet. Laughing, falling, rolling helplessly down its side, Christina felt sixteen again and deliriously happy. She ended up in a breathless heap at the bottom. Daniel managed a more dignified, if no less hasty, exit. He knelt beside her, brushing sand from her face and hair.

"Are you all right?" he asked sharply.

"I'm wonderful!" she exulted, laughing up at him with all the joy she felt. Daniel sucked in his breath, his face so close she could feel the sharp exhalation as their eyes met and clung, and the tiny space between them suddenly sang with tension. Her laughter stilled as the hands yet brushing sand from her hair thrust deep into its satiny softness and pulled her mouth to his in a hard, urgent kiss.

Although her heart gave an astonishing leap, Christina could pinpoint no particular sensation beyond the rough, demanding pressure of his lips. It was so brief, Daniel was on his feet and stretching out a hand to her before she had time to catch her breath.

"Time to go," he said tightly.

His face closed and set, Daniel brushed himself off and rolled down his sleeves as if the act signaled an end to playtime. Christina lowered her head and set her own self to rights, her mind still hung up on the startling kiss. It had seemingly given him no pleasure. A meaningless impulse, quickly done and as quickly regretted, she supposed. Obviously not something to be discussed—but certainly something to wonder about.

He was so remote and preoccupied on the drive back to the airport that attempts at conversation seemed pointless. Once aboard the plane, he opened his briefcase, and as easily as that he was again the daunting stranger.

Christina studied him with avid curiosity. This lovely afternoon might not have happened and his kiss been just a figment of her imagination. She shook her head with wonder and curled up for a much needed nap.

Daniel shook her awake. "We'll be landing soon— fasten your seat belt, sleepyhead," he ordered gruffly. Still half asleep, Christina began fumbling for the displaced straps. "Oh, here, let me do that," he growled. Bending over her, he searched out the belt and quickly fastened it.

The hard knuckles on her soft belly aroused a flare of intensely sensual warmth. Uneasily, Christina shifted against their disturbing touch. The dark head lifted—and froze in place. Her warm, sleep-flushed face and drowsy eyes were framed by a wind-tossed romp of silky black hair. Unaware of how desirable she looked to the man whose mouth hovered just above hers, Christina gazed into dark, emerald eyes lit by an inner fire.

His fingers clenched against her soft flesh as they stared at each other. Daniel leaned so close his cool breath brushed her lips, and for an electrifying moment they were again caught up in the force of a taut, throbbing tension. It enveloped them like a shimmering web.

Swiftly Daniel stepped back from her. Inscrutable green eyes spared a glance at her rosy face as he sat down and snapped on his seat belt. "By the way, it isn't on your agenda, but we're attending a formal party in San Antonio tonight. You do have a gown with you?" Still struggling with confusion, she shook her head. "All right," he sighed. "You'll have time to pick up something. I do hope we won't have to shop at every hotel we hit. You're to be prepared for any contingency, Miss Lacey. Always an evening gown—and a pair of slacks. I strongly suggest you not be caught unprepared again."

"That's very unfair, Mr. Belmont," she reproved. "I was unprepared because I was uninformed. And why must *I* attend this party?"

Daniel's prolonged look out the window was surprisingly near a delaying tactic. It was her first time to see him without a prompt response. Puzzled, she openly watched him. When he faced her again, his expression was unreadable, but she had the impression of a man at odds with himself. She wondered suddenly if he was recalling the kiss, but decided not; he had brushed it off as easily as he brushed the sand from his trouser cuffs.

"Because I want you there," Daniel said. "That should suffice, shouldn't it?"

One did not argue with that tone of voice. He could so easily disarm her, it would be the height of idiocy to even consider giving vent to the resentment he evoked. "Yes, sir," said Christina smartly.

The plane landed and Daniel stood up and stretched like a sleek cat. He paused, studying her disheveled appearance as she came to her feet. A smile of piercing sweetness lit his dark face. "Are you quite sure three hours will be sufficient time to make yourself presentable, Miss Lacey?" he asked dubiously.

Never knowing when to take him seriously, Christina shrugged. "I'll do my best, Mr. Belmont," she solemnly assured.

"What more can a man ask?" Daniel murmured. His direct gaze seemed to issue a deliberate challenge as he carelessly added, "Oh, by the way, the party is at Lisa Manning's house. Eight o'clock. I'll be arriving earlier, so you'll have to take a cab. Any questions, Miss Lacey?"

"No, no questions," said Christina.

Chapter Three

Contrary to her cool denial, Christina was dying of curiosity. Why did he need her at Lisa Manning's party? After hastily selecting a gown and accessories from the hotel boutique, she washed and dried her hair while pondering her mystery. Knowing his respect for her gifted perceptions, it was possible he intended making use of them tonight. But the festive atmosphere of a party was hardly conducive to business.

Christina let the matter drop. Attending Lisa's party was decidedly *not* her idea of pleasure. However, since Daniel gave her no options, she would consider herself still on duty and act accordingly.

So resolved, Christina annointed her throat and temples with a sweet, dusky fragrance, then carefully began dressing. Although of an eye-catching hue, the gown she had purchased was exquisitely simple, merely a supple length of fabric that clung to her curvacious figure, winding over one shoulder and leaving the other enticingly bare to the embrace of a satiny black curl.

Stepping back to survey the results, Christina's eyes flew wide with pleased surprise. The mirror revealed a startlingly appealing woman. Would he notice? "With Lisa Manning on his arm? Really, Christina," she said aloud, deriding herself.

The confident air she assumed was admittedly a trifle shaky, but it lasted all the way to Lisa's elegant white mansion. A rather daunting butler escorted Christina to an enormous room overlooking an equally large terrace elegant with flowers and Japanese lanterns and splendidly dressed people. Her breath caught in her throat as she spied Daniel. Relaxed and superbly at ease in what was to her a formidable gathering, he was heart-stoppingly sensuous in formal attire. Just looking at him was an incomparable pleasure.

Shy and uncertain, Christina's heart went completely haywire as Daniel glanced up and saw her. No woman could mistake his heady male reaction—even when it was replaced by an indulgent smile that practically patted her on the head.

Her fragile elation was shattered at the sight of the woman who attached herself to Daniel's arm with insouciant possessiveness. Iridescent gray eyes and a swirl of sunset hair, Lisa Manning in the flesh was literally breathtaking. She could not compete with such a creature, Christina bleakly admitted, neither in looks nor the sophistication Lisa wore like a sleek second skin.

Realizing she was thinking like a woman rather than a glorified secretary, Christina gave herself a brisk mental shake. She'd known tonight wouldn't be pleasant, hadn't she? Coolly she smiled and extended her hand. "Miss Manning," she said. "It's a pleasure to meet you."

In truth Christina hadn't known what to expect tonight, but it certainly wasn't hours of watching Daniel interact with another woman or this prickly, almost painful constriction of heart. Unaware that what she felt was jealousy, she chattered and danced and smiled until her mouth ached.

At midnight Christina decided she'd had enough of it. Courteously she thanked Lisa for the privilege of enduring this excruciating pleasure, although she didn't word it *quite* that way.

To her dismay, Daniel insisted on driving her back to the hotel.

"Really, Mr. Belmont, there's no need—I can taxi back to the hotel," she protested as he started the car.

"Oh, nonsense—it's only a short drive, Miss Lacey," Daniel said.

Christina noted anew his odd habit of overusing her name, as if he derived some peculiar pleasure from saying it.

Noting her quick shiver, Daniel turned on the heater. "Did you enjoy the party?" he asked nicely.

Christina stifled a sarcastic laugh. He had favored her with precisely one dance, and that so impersonal she had resented rather than enjoyed it. When it ended, he thanked her, escorted her back to their table, and laughingly scooped up Lisa for a hot, throbbing disco number. The two of them had shared her table when they weren't dancing cheek to cheek or playing the elegant hosts.

Remembering her constricted yearning as she watched them together, Christina cleared her throat and belatedly answered Daniel's question. "The party was lovely, and I enjoyed it very much," she said firmly.

"And Greg Stafford?"

She glanced at the handsome profile, noting his rigid set of jaw. Greg Stafford was the attractive, fortyish, well-to-do companion Lisa had thoughtfully provided for the evening. Christina had found him comfortable, if not exactly thrilling. As for Greg, he had been openly enchanted with his "charming little wild flower." Her mouth twisted. Wild flower indeed!

She gave a throaty little laugh. "And especially Greg Stafford. Lisa Manning did me a very nice favor, in fact," she mused, wondering at Lisa's motives.

"Didn't she, though. By the way, one rule I feel I must enforce—you do not make dates on my time," Daniel said mildly.

Furiously offended, Christina bit down on her lip. Greg lived in Corpus, and he had merely asked to call her. "I thought your time ended at five o'clock," she remarked.

"My time ends when I say it ends."

The cutting response nullified any further desire to speak. She was stung and confused and very near tears. Her present mood was in direct response to his, but what had angered *him?* With icy reserve Christina folded her hands and stared straight ahead during the remainder of the drive.

When they were at last standing in front of her door, Daniel held out his hand for the key. He followed her inside and closed the door sharply behind him. Too spent to heed the smoldering green eyes watching her with a dangerous glint, she looked up at him in weary annoyance.

"Mr. Belmont, surely my duties are ended for the night?"

His hands snaked out and caught her shoulders. "Not yet, Miss Lacey, not yet," he said with razor-edged softness. Daniel hauled her against his chest so suddenly, she had no time to react.

Christina's shocked cry was smothered by the mouth pressing on hers, forcing her lips apart for the thrusting plunder of his tongue, demanding the response he wanted. His arms curved around her, tightening until she was trapped like a moth against his dizzying warmth, until her breasts were crushed into the unyielding strength of his chest and she could feel his heart thudding as violently as her own!

Each movement she made was countered with a tensing of the steel bonds holding her helplessly captive; each time she tried to twist free, his kiss simply deepened. And she was fighting herself now, struggling against the wave of fiery excitement thundering through her blood, coming sweetly on her lips as his kiss grew more passionate. She had never been kissed like this before, never known anything like this all-pervasive warmth weakening her legs until she would have fallen had he released her.

Her hands moved of their own accord and tangled deep in his hair. His mouth lifted from hers to move hungrily across her face, down her throat, over her naked shoulder in a trail of fire that blazed all through her—every inch of her! "Like satin," he whispered, his tongue a velvet rasp on her naked skin. She wound her arms around him in mindless discovery of the sweet, sweet fire of his straining body.

Daniel slid his hands down the silky length of her spine in a soft, sensuous caress that made her tremble and forced a moan from her lips as he held and touched and explored. "Christina," he whispered, the first time she had heard her name spoken so. Warm and thrillingly possessive, his rough mouth moved over her face, seeking her lips, taking her breath with his deep and sensual kiss, a wild, impassioned rapture that went on and on while her senses were deliciously spinning . . .

Daniel released her so abruptly she clutched at him to keep her balance. Eyes as soft and tender as the flowers they resembled stared at him in stunned confusion. For an instant she thought he looked as stunned as she felt, but his expression changed so swiftly she didn't know what she saw.

His hands moved to her shoulders again, as if to hold her away from him. The gleam of hot green eyes seared her skin as he suddenly laughed. "Your immunity seems to have slipped a notch, Miss Lacey," he softly taunted.

Shocked, outraged, humiliated, and so many other things that she could not even begin to name, Christina stood rigid as he inclined his head in a mocking salute and sauntered out the door. Savagely she bit back her fierce urge to call out to him. She could not reveal this churning confusion she felt!

After closing the door and methodically locking it, she stepped out of the lovely gown with the same blank-faced attention to detail. Only when she had completed her nightly ritual and was safely in bed would she give in to it.

The moonlight made dancing patterns on the ceiling. She lay wide-eyed and painfully confused. It had meant nothing to him. She had been utterly overwhelmed by his fiery kisses, and even now her body throbbed with unfulfilled desire—and it meant absolutely *nothing* to him. He was undoubtedly back at Windchase by now with Lisa.

Christina pressed the back of her hand against her mouth to stifle a sob. She would not cry, she viciously admonished herself. *She would not cry.*

To her surprise, Christina slept late the next morning. Daniel probably did too, she thought spitefully. No telling what time he'd gotten in last night! Aggravated at herself for falling back into this trap immediately upon awakening, she shoved all thoughts of his extracurricular activities from her mind. No more analyzing, no more searching through each moment of the evening for clues to explain his behavior—just no more!

After a quick wake-up shower, she put on a yellow blouse and slacks, stuck her feet into sandals, tied her hair back, and sat down to await his summons. The schedule had been left blank today, so she assumed they would return to Corpus.

Unable to sit for long, she began pacing the room, one hand on her hip and the other rubbing the back of her neck. Why had he kissed her? Just to test her immunity? Then why had he stopped? Why not test it further! Remembering too clearly for comfort her uninhibited response, she shuddered.

"Oh, now, Christina," she scoffed aloud. It had been presumptuous of her to suppose she was immune to that devastating charm he possessed in such abundance, but now that she knew just how susceptible she was, she would be on guard in the future. That made sense, she thought, cautiously examining it. Perhaps last night he had actually done her a favor by shocking her to awareness of her vulnerability. . . .

Christina jumped at the sharp rap. Hurriedly pasting a smile on her face, she opened the door.

"Good morning! Have you had breakfast?" Daniel asked.

"No, I just woke up. You slept late too—and you look tired. Late hours last night?" she couldn't resist asking.

"Miss Lacey, I'm in a good mood this morning. Please don't spoil it. Come, let's have breakfast," he chided with a charming smile.

Refusing to be charmed, Christina ignored it. "I assume I won't have to keep your coffee cup filled at breakfast?" she snapped.

"You look like sunshine in that outfit," replied Daniel.

His infuriatingly good mood persisted throughout the enormous breakfast he ordered. Christina seethed as she studied what she could see of him over a newspaper. He had made no reference to last night. Well, she could wait, but they were damn well going to discuss it!

"Why are you glowering at me, Miss Lacey?" Daniel asked, lowering his paper.

Christina lay aside the butter knife clenched in her hand. "Mr. Belmont, I would like to say something —and I'd appreciate your undivided attention, if you please. I do not approve of games between employer and employee," she said assertively, although she wasn't quite certain she'd worded it as precisely as she intended.

Daniel gave a judicious nod. "I applaud your good sense. Would you like part of the paper?"

An hour or so later they were on the plane headed for Corpus Christi. Christina's anger returned full force as Daniel promptly immersed himself in paperwork. She felt secretly relieved that he had refused to discuss last night's episode and incensed that he could ignore it.

"Miss Lacey, I really am getting tired of those stabbing looks. Is something wrong?" he glanced up to inquire.

"You know there is," she rebuked.

"May I inquire what?" he asked, resignedly patient.

"Mr. Belmont, you know perfectly well what's wrong."

"If I knew, I wouldn't be asking, would I?" he countered.

Christina took a deep breath. "Last night."

"Last night . . . ah, I am enlightened at last. Miss Lacey, I think you're overreacting. It was just a kiss."

"In my opinion, it was far from just a kiss," she retorted.

He shrugged. "If you wish to fantasize, I suppose that's your privilege." His head lowered again.

An appalling possibility—had she overreacted? Fantasized even? Christina clenched her hands. "You're a cold-blooded snake," she muttered.

"Really? I've certainly never thought of myself as cold-blooded," he remarked idly.

"Don't you care what I think of you?" she asked after a small silence.

Daniel did not look up. "Not particularly, no."

"Or anyone else?" she snapped.

He lay down his pen with one of his long-suffering sighs. "Miss Lacey—"

"If you say 'Miss Lacey' like that again, I shall come across this table and assault you," Christina grimly promised.

"Heavens!" Daniel murmured. An eyebrow quirked. "Am I wrong, or have you not been impressed at the size of my business?"

"Well, yes, but I hardly see—"

"How do you think it came to be so impressive? Not by excessive sensitivity to what others might think of me. Not by being kind and considerate, not by being warm-blooded . . . businesswise, I mean," he said with a quick, adorable grin.

"All right, Mr. Belmont, how did it get to be so impressive?" she intoned, wishing she weren't so interested in the answer.

"It got so impressive because I took what wits I have and I used them eighteen hours a day, seven days a week, fifty-two weeks a year for ten years. In short, I worked my damn fool head off getting where I am today, and I think you'll agree that I'm still dedicated to the task?"

Christina wilted in the face of that volley. "Yes, I have to admit—I know you work hard, Mr. Belmont."

"Thank you," Daniel snapped. Studying her confused face, his voice softened to devastating gentleness. "Last night was just a kiss, Miss Lacey. If it was so unpleasant, I humbly apologize, and I'll make certain it doesn't happen again—not without undue provocation, at any rate." Humor lit his eyes. "Now, may I get back to work?"

"Yes, sir," said Christina. Considerably chastened, she sat back and stared reflectively out the window. Why hadn't she just let the matter go? In retrospect it seemed much the more sensible course to follow. A sophisticated woman would have shrugged it off as an occupational hazard (her sense of humor asserted itself). Some sophisticated woman she was, magnifying just a kiss all out of proportion! All her pacing and brooding boiled down to an exercise in futility.

When she looked up with a rueful smile sweetening her lips, Daniel was watching her. He snapped shut the file and replaced it, then began massaging his shoulders. The long fringes of his lashes were like silky dark fans, she thought. As his fingers pressed she caught the grimace of pain.

"Stiff neck?" she asked.

"Yeah," he muttered.

Christina had often seen that look on her mother's face after a bad night and it touched her deeply. Impulsively she unbuckled her seat belt and got to her feet. "My mother had problems with her neck and back. Sometimes I could help relieve it—may I?" she asked diffidently. Ignoring his startled look, she walked around behind him and replaced his fingers with hers. "Take off your tie and unbutton your collar," she ordered.

"Yes, ma'am," he said.

Christina was still a little surprised at her audacity, but she did have talented hands and the skill to apply them; Dave had taught her well. That Dave had been a handy man to have around, she thought drolly. Her fingers stilled for an instant. How odd that she could think of him with nothing but affection. Digging gently into knotted muscles, her slim hands began the magic her good friend had taught her.

Daniel's long sigh of pleasure warmed her heart. Following an impulse she did not understand, Christina lowered her head and brushed his hair with a kiss so fleeting he wasn't aware of it. His hair smelled fresh and clean and was soft as silk under her lips. Methodically she continued the massage, beginning to feel somewhat uneasy at her forwardness. He might misconstrue her genuine desire to help.

Daniel leaned his head back on her wrists and looked up at her, an eyebrow slanting in quizzical regard as her fingers stilled again.

"Does that feel better?" she asked.

"That feels wonderful. A spot here, though . . ."

Positioning her thumbs in the center of his neck, she said, "Now, bend your head, slowly lean away from, and then back into, the point of pressure . . . slowly," she stressed.

"Ummm," he sighed. "Where did you learn this?" Daniel asked curiously.

"From Dave."

"Ah, yes, Dave. Who was that mysterious, multitalented man, hm?"

"Not such a mystery. He was an older man I kept company with for a time. A very good friend, actually," Christina reflected. "During the last months of my mother's illness, Dave was always there when I needed someone. A very good friend," she reaffirmed.

"How long was your mother ill?" Daniel asked quietly.

Her fingers moved rhythmically over his neck and

shoulders. "Mother was never a physically strong woman. She had a spinal defect that gave her intense pain at times. But unless one knew her very well, like me, you'd never know she was suffering. She was . . . brave," Christina said softly. As if to herself, she continued in this vein, relating her mother's travail with pride for such magnificent courage.

"You say she became incapacitated when you were sixteen. Who took care of her? And you?" Daniel queried.

"My aunt and uncle—Pauline is Mother's older sister. And friends, neighbors, the church—and me, of course. We got along. Is your mother still alive?"

"No. My parents were divorced when I was nine. I lived with my father. Mother remarried shortly after the divorce and moved away. She and her new husband were killed two years later—plane crash," he said matter-of-factly.

"It must have been rough," she murmured.

"As you said, we got along," Daniel said.

Inexpressibly stirred, her fingers became caressing for a moment. How strange that last night she had hated him so fiercely she ached to strike back, and now she was coping with tenderness. "Your father— what sort of man was he?" she softly dared.

In the deep breath he released Christina sensed a relaxing of guard. Suddenly they were close; up here in the clouds they were intensely alone.

Daniel folded his strong hands on the table. "Dad was quiet, soft-spoken—busy, of course, but he always had time for me." He glanced at the white mist of cloud they were passing through. "In early spring we used to go to this place in Canada, a wild, primitive, very lonely place. We had an old cabin, a small runabout . . . some mornings the air was utterly blue, so cold and crisp you could taste it on your tongue . . ."

He spoke with a bemused lilt, and Christina listened enrapt as he went on relating what were obviously his fondest memories. Suddenly he stopped short and flexed his arms, saying, "Well, that was all a long time ago."

"I hope the massage helped," she said, taking her seat again.

Testingly he wriggled his shoulders. "Yes, very much so. I thank you, Miss Lacey." The smile he slanted at her deliberately mocked those few moments of closeness. "Perhaps your hidden talents outshine your more obvious ones," he drawled.

Taking her hand, he studied the fingers so sweetly small and feminine in contrast to his male strength. His sooty lashes fanned down. "Very talented fingers," he murmured to himself.

Sensing his turn of thought, Christina withdrew from him and fixed her gaze out the window. Corpus Christi lay below, shining whitely in the noonday sun. She was glad to be home, she thought. Her expressive face softened into lines of wistfulness as she watched the scene below. It was the first time she had thought of this city as home.

When they arrived at the office, Christina and Daniel took up the voluminous correspondence that had piled up in his absence. They worked steadily. At times like this she felt so in tune with his mind that the unspoken communication between them was more satisfying than any conversation.

At three he glanced at his watch, then at the slim figure walking to the file cabinet. Unaware of his scrutiny, Christina replaced the file and paused to rub her dully throbbing temples.

"Why don't you take the rest of the afternoon off—I can finish up here," Daniel absently suggested. "It's been a long day."

It felt deliciously soothing to enter the shabby rooms that were nonetheless her own cozy sanctuary. Christina sank down on the couch and confessed to a bone-deep weariness. By the time she'd managed the requisite trip to the supermarket, she was visibly drooping; by eight o'clock she was tucked under her grandmother's tulip-patterned quilt blissfully asleep.

The next morning she lay propped up in bed with a tray table and the newspaper at hand, feeling at peace with the entire world, Daniel Belmont included. Idly, she scanned the front page, then thumbed through looking for the society column and the expected picture of Daniel and Lisa.

Coffee sloshed her fingers as her own face leaped out at her. Not Daniel and Lisa—Daniel and *Christina!* At Windchase, Lisa Manning's palatial home. When during the evening had the picture been taken? And why, she wondered angrily, had it been so prominently displayed in the society column?

"Lovely secretary," she read aloud. There had been oblique references to Daniel Belmont's attractive secretary in the papers before, but this was somehow different. She was now elevated to "lovely secretary," and she tasted an obscure note of snideness in the comment.

Maybe she was making too much of this. She had known when she accepted this job that speculation would accompany it, but her mother's teachings had taken firm root; if you know yourself to be innocent of wrongdoing, then unjust accusation can be disregarded.

But not easily, Christina sighingly admitted. She was revolted at the thought of being considered Daniel's mistress, just another of a long string of such conquests. *Especially when it's not true,* she thought.

However, it was not just her pride smarting, or even mere feminine vanity, although both figured heavily in her altered mood. Christina knew the fragility of a reputation. Once tarnished, the stain was indelible, and someday there would be a special man who valued his wife's good name as much as she did.

It really was a fine-honed choice, Christina flatly conceded. She could stop now, before the gossip became vicious, or she could continue in her present position and accept the consequences.

Not for an instant would she give up Daniel Belmont because of possible damage to her reputation! Shocked at her vehement thought, Christina frantically amended, "I meant give up my position, of course—it has nothing to do with Daniel as a man!"

And since she was innocent of wrongdoing, she told herself smartly, she would hold her head high above malicious speculation.

Nevertheless, she was subdued and given to monosyllabic responses when she reported for work Monday. Daniel was shortly leaving for Egypt and had no time for idle chitchat. As if he were given to such, she thought, flashing a resentful look at the figure hunched over a stack of files.

"Miss Lacey, why am I being stabbed again?" Daniel inquired.

Good grief, did he have eyes in the back of his head? "Sorry. Here's the workup on Oshman, Ltd," she responded just as briefly.

"All right, what is it now?" he asked with that maddening air of patience.

"If you must know, that column bothered me a trifle," she snapped. He looked so puzzled, Christina said, "You know—the picture?"

"The picture?"

"Don't you read the society column?" she asked incredulously.

"I never read the society column," said Daniel.

Christina unsnapped her purse and took out the clipping. "Well, do me a favor and read it this time," she ordered.

Daniel scanned it with galling lack of interest.

"Well?" she prompted.

"Very nice. You look pretty."

She blushed at the idiotic pleasure his reply engendered. *"Read* it!"

As though indulging a precocious child, Daniel read it. "It says we were photographed at Lisa's party. Should I sue?"

"Mr. Belmont, would you please put aside sarcasm and try to discuss this in a sensible, even compassionate manner?"

Daniel checked his watch. "I hope this isn't going to take long. My plane leaves in—"

"I *know* when your plane leaves. I . . ." A wave of disappointment swept over her. How stupid to hope for understanding—what did he care about her reputation! "Oh, forget it. I'm sorry I said anything," Christina said dully. Straightening her shoulders, she picked up a sheaf of papers and began sorting them to order.

A finger suddenly slid under her chin and turned her face to his. "Miss Lacey, please sit down," Daniel said gently, huskily. "It's time we had a talk."

Chapter Four

Surprised at this abrupt shift, Christina sank down in the chair facing his desk. Daniel perched on the edge of it and raked a hand through his rumpled hair. The gentleness in his eyes absolved his sigh, she decided.

"Now. We really don't have much time—certainly not enough to waste over a matter like this," he said, the cutting edge returning to his voice as he flicked the clipping aside. "I think you're overreacting, Miss Lacey. It's merely a picture of Daniel Belmont and his secretary—"

"*Lovely* secretary," she corrected.

"All right, so they exaggerate—gossip columnists usually do," he dryly agreed. "At any rate, a tender skin is something you simply cannot afford in your job. You must have known there would be speculation—I told you before that reporters take an inordinate interest in my personal life. I've learned to ignore it, and so must you. Any type of gossip is best ignored. That's the only way to express your contempt."

"I'm well aware of that, but this particular sort of gossip galls me. It only enhances your reputation, but mine—I happen to despise being thought of as your mistress when I haven't had the pleasure!" Christina said hotly. Her unfortunate choice of words sent her heart plummeting to her toes. The sudden deviltry in his eyes did nothing to help. Daniel got up with a grin tucking into his lips.

"Why, I suppose that would be galling," he said in an unctuous voice. "How rude of me—how inconsiderate and *arrogant*—to deny you that pleasure. Unfortunately, I do have this trip." He sighed again. Lounging on the corner of the desk, he let his gaze wander down her. "But as soon as I return—"

"Oh, shut up! I might have known you'd react like that," she said bitterly.

"Miss Lacey, listen to me." All trace of mockery vanished as he grasped her chin and raised her face to his level gaze. "It's going to get worse, not better. Once it begins, it never retreats. You have to face that fact, and you might as well start now. What others think doesn't matter. Remember that, Miss Lacey. Just trust your own instincts—the rest is totally irrelevant," he said softly, fiercely, as if to himself.

His words stirred her deeply. "My mother told me something like that," she confided.

Daniel's lips brushed her nose before he drew back to say, "Your mother was a wise woman. Now, can we get back to work?"

Christina sighed. "Yes, I suppose you're right about the gossip. I'll do my best to ignore it."

"Oh, by the way, you may take the next few days off since I won't be needing you. Mrs. Coyle can handle things. Now where's that Oshman workup? And that communiqué from London—I can't find it anywhere," he said aggrievedly, rifling the papers on his desktop.

Christina suddenly wanted to put her arms around him and hug him—just *hug* him. "Here it is, Mr. Belmont," she said, unable to suppress a chuckle.

He looked at her sternly, but a grin twitched his mouth and spoiled it. "Humph. . . . Is that meeting with Cairo confirmed? Who typed this? There are two errors on this page alone. Haven't I a decent typist in the lot? Didn't you even bother to check this, Miss Lacey?"

Feeling absurdly happy, Christina bustled around and got things straightened out. She drove him to the airport. Business to the very last second, she thought, mentally shaking her head at his stamina.

"Something?" Daniel asked, cocking an eyebrow.

"No, nothing. Have a good time in Egypt, Mr. Belmont."

"Um, I imagine I will," he agreed. "Well, against all odds, here we are. No good-bye kiss?"

"Certainly not. That isn't one of my duties," she said crisply.

He grinned. "I may make it one." Daniel caught her chin and set his mouth on hers. Christina refused to acknowledge the insolently casual kiss. "Hm. You need practice," he advised. "Good-bye, Miss Lacey. Drive carefully."

"Good-bye, Mr. Belmont. I hope a camel steps on your foot," she called out sweetly.

The rich, husky sound of his laughter seemed to linger in her ears for days afterward. Christina was appalled at how keenly she missed Daniel Belmont during his absence. It's like winter, she thought. Dull, gray, without a ray of sunshine.

She spent several evenings with Greg Stafford, but this did little to lift her unaccountable depression. Her days were devoid of excitement and incredibly long. Every minute was laced with an odd sense of waiting.

When she returned from her coffee break Monday afternoon and saw Daniel sitting behind his desk, his face expressionless, his beautiful green eyes making their brief, intense appraisal of her dress and the slender body in it, she could not contain her joyous smile.

"Good afternoon, Mr. Belmont!" she caroled.

His mask split. "Good afternoon, Miss Lacey."

That was it, she thought happily. No one had called her Miss Lacey like that in four whole days!

Daniel frowned severely. "Well, are we going to stand here smiling at each other or are we going to work?" he asked sourly.

"Yes, sir. Sorry, sir," she said with lilting impudence.

Maintaining his frown despite another twitch of lips, Daniel removed his jacket, then pulled off his tie and rolled back his cuffs. Christina handed him the sorted mail, with several personal letters— including one from Lisa Manning—on top. He set them aside with a negligent glance absurdly pleasing to Christina, and they soon began working in flawless harmony. They were a perfectly matched team when it came to work, she thought with pride.

The afternoon hours flew by unheeded. It was after six when Daniel paused to fix a drink. Christina settled back in her chair and flexed her cramped fingers. That it was past quitting time was irrelevant; she felt content right where she was.

Regarding her over the rim of his glass, he casually inquired. "You seeing much of Stafford these days?" When she hesitated, he lifted a sardonic eyebrow. "I withdraw the question if it's out of line."

"Yes, I see a lot of him," she slowly replied.

"No one else?"

"No one else."

"Why not?"

Taken aback at his sharpening tone, Christina stammered, "Why I—I just haven't. Greg's company is—is adequate."

Daniel studied her with glinting mockery. "Adequate. I'd certainly hate to hear myself described as adequate," he remarked.

Christina sucked in her breath as his gaze caught hers and held with disturbing intensity. For an electrifying moment identities receded; they were man and woman and each keenly aware of it. The scent of him set her pulses racing, and she had a fierce, urgent longing to kiss that sensual smile. Again she was sharply reminded of just how susceptible she was to the attraction he so effortlessly exerted. Well, forewarned is forearmed, she thought, breaking the unnerving contact by sheer will.

Ignoring his faintly taunting laugh, she snapped open a folder. "I think we'd best get back to work—I don't relish the thought of being here all night," she suggested crisply.

"The conscientious Miss Lacey," Daniel murmured with a cryptic smile. He sat back down at his desk. "All right, give me the cost estimates first."

Christina crossed her legs, but she could have been a typewriter for all the interest in his flat gaze. They were back to work with a vengeance.

As routine days flowed smoothly into a month free of disturbing incidents, Christina began to feel secure both in herself and her job. She had an established routine, a fairly enjoyable social life, and an optimistic outlook on the future.

In this pleasant frame of mind she strolled into the reception room one rain-misted morning to find the two office girls clustered around Mrs. Coyle's desk, reading a newspaper over her shoulder. Wondering at their attentive gazes, Christina smiled a greeting and headed for Daniel's door.

"He isn't in yet," Mrs. Coyle said. "Have you seen this?" she asked, tapping the newspaper.

Not another picture! Christina sighed to herself. "No, I overslept this morning, didn't have time to do more than scan the front page. What is it?" she asked, joining them.

Standing behind the plump shoulder, she read the red-penciled item. "Beautiful Lisa Manning surprised her pals by announcing her upcoming nuptials to Daniel Belmont, one of Corpus Christi's leading citizens. When put to the question, Miss Manning coyly explained they had not yet set the date. Friends predict it will be *the* social event of the season, and this reporter certainly agrees with that!"

Feeling as though she had been punched in the belly, Christina couldn't think for a moment. Shaken by her intense inner reaction, knowing that others were watching her, she kept a poker face. "Well, this surely comes as no surprise to anyone. I mean, you've known for months that they— Oh, good morning, Mr. Belmont!" she broke off, flushing as he strode in the door.

"Good morning, ladies," Daniel said with a brief smile. "Miss Lacey, if you please?"

Christina followed him through the door and closed it behind her.

"Will you draw the shades, please? The sun seems overly bright this morning," Daniel muttered accusingly.

"Hangover, Mr. Belmont?" she sweetly inquired.

"Don't provoke me, Miss Lacey," he warned.

"Sorry," she murmured, lowering the shades against the sunlight.

Giving her a grim look, he sat down behind his desk and picked up the mail. Christina sat down opposite him and crossed her legs, swinging one foot in cool indifference to his morning examination.

"You have something to say, do you, Miss Lacey?" he asked sourly.

"No, sir, I was just . . . well, I suppose I should say congratulations—"

"Congratulations?" he cut in with an ominous look.

Undaunted, she continued. "Congratulations on your upcoming nuptials to Miss Manning."

Daniel's laugh came mostly through his nose. "You don't seem too happy about that, Miss Lacey," he observed.

"I? Nonsense. It occurs to me *you* don't seem too happy about it."

"My happiness is not open to discussion," he said testily.

His eyes were so hard and cold, Christina shivered. He could be so forbidding! Still very much shaken by the announcement, she responded with slicing sarcasm. "Do excuse my rudeness, Mr. Belmont, but I just happened to think your office staff could offer congratulations without getting their heads snapped off!"

"If I want congratulations, I'll send out a memo," Daniel said. A glint of cold amusement flickered in his eyes. "Besides, haven't I advised you against heeding gossip?"

Gazing into the sparkling green eyes, Christina protested, "Yes, you have, but this is hardly gossip."

"Miss Manning is entitled to her opinion. However, it does not necessarily reflect mine," Daniel drawled.

Christina went weak with relief at this disclaimer, a most irritating reaction. Why should it matter whether or not they were engaged? Catching his oddly intent perusal, she shrugged a slim shoulder, which proclaimed his romantic affairs no concern of hers.

"What's the matter, Miss Lacey? Were you a trifle piqued that I hadn't added you to my trophy shelf before being, shall we say, taken out of action?" he taunted.

"Oh, don't be stupid," she said with massive disdain.

"Stupid?"

"Yes, stupid. You let your success go to your head, Mr. Belmont. Not every woman finds you irresistible, you know." Christina heard her own voice with a growing sense of despair. He was drawing her into another ridiculous argument. Why did she rise to the bait like a largemouth bass!

"They don't?" Daniel asked with surprise.

"No, they don't! I myself find your so-called

charms about as irresistible as a case of the Hong Kong flu!"

"Do you now," he said, dangerously soft.

Horrified at what she'd said, Christina stepped back as he came out of his chair. She had known he was in no mood for defiance—why on earth had she challenged him!

"Excuse me, I'll get the files," she said, and started toward the door.

"The files can wait, Miss Lacey." Daniel's steely voice stopped her. Christina turned and gave a little cry of surprise as she bumped into a very solid chest. Without warning, his hands thrust into her hair and crushed her mouth on his.

At first too outraged to heed the warmth surging through her, Christina shoved furiously at his shoulders. But his hands left her hair and spread across her back, pressing her into him until the warmth between them became leaping flames. Some part of her cried out in shock as she became aware of his exploring hands, but the rest of Christina Lacey melted against his lean hard frame in mindless delight.

His kiss sweetened with passion as Daniel sensed her surrender to the moment. Without her volition, her arms wound tightly around his neck. She knew his every caress was a deliberate assault on her reeling senses, but it didn't matter. Nothing mattered but the fiery delight of the mouth hungrily devouring hers, the intoxicating pleasure of the hands expertly roaming her body. They curved around her hips and roughly strained her into him, and the thin, silken fabric of her dress was the only flimsy barrier between her body and those long, seductive fingers.

Christina shuddered at the electric sensations pulsing from his flesh to hers and back again to wind around them like molten ribbons. Mindlessly she pressed closer. His fingers seemed to burn through her dress and she realized with a shock of dismay that she wanted—*wanted*—to feel them hot and intimate on her naked skin.

His mouth lifted from hers just long enough to murmur, "The Hong Kong flu, Miss Lacey?"

Loathing the sarcasm in his voice, she still could not remove her fingers from his thick hair. Aching to kiss him again, Christina knew a wild sense of desolation when he pulled away from her clinging arms to regard her with arrogant satisfaction. Her mind whirled, but the one outstanding fact she grasped was the appalling knowledge that he had kissed her with the confident assurance of a man who knew full well she lied.

Shame scalded her at the amusement gleaming in his narrowed gaze. Christina clenched her hands until her nails cut deep into her tender palms. Several deep breaths were required to steady herself, and if she did not find an alternate emotion stronger than her shame, she was going to burst into tears!

Her eyes flashed fire as she found that alternative. Christina tilted her head and laughed. "Don't look so triumphant, Mr. Belmont," she drawled. "It's just natural, even instinctive, for a female to respond to an attractive man. Oh, yes, I admit you're attractive. But so is the office boy on the tenth floor. The reaction would have been the same—perhaps more so. He's exceedingly young and handsome."

Although she could not begin to guess which one, she sensed her soft taunt had struck a dangerous nerve. The strong features perceptibly tightened and a hot light flared in his eyes. Christina stepped back in genuine alarm as he began moving toward her with slow, deliberate purpose, an icy smile curving his mouth. She had provoked him far beyond her intentions!

"A remarkable theory, Miss Lacy. But one I'm disinclined to believe," he said mockingly.

Christina took one look at those turbulent green eyes and turned to flee. Too late, she tried to move away from him, but he caught her arm and spun her around to kiss her again. She felt herself weakly succumbing to the heat of his lips, the strong embrace, and the sweet torture of his tongue forcing her lips apart and probing the honeyed cave of her mouth while his hands etched trails of sensuous fire down the trembling length of her spine. Her response might be instinctive as she claimed, but it was overwhelmingly strong. Powerless to prevent it, raging at herself even while it was happening, Christina yielded to the pounding urgency softening her body to velvet in his arms.

He withdrew his mouth from hers with tantalizing slowness and moved around the desk. Except for his escalated breathing, Daniel betrayed no visible signs of having just kissed a woman with passionate intensity. When Mrs. Coyle rang, he dispassionately answered, listened, and issued instructions that struck Christina's ears as meaningless garble.

She had remained exactly where he had left her, incapable of willing her limbs to move. Releasing the intercom button, Daniel looked up impatiently, an eyebrow winging up in studied surprise at her stillness.

"You said . . . this would not happen again," she whispered.

"There's an amendment to that—not unless you provoke me. And you did provoke me, Miss Lacey. Now get the Hamilton file, please?" he coolly requested. An unpleasant smile thinned his lips. "It's in Records, on the tenth floor."

Christina lowered her head to the stinging threat of tears. The kiss that had utterly shattered her was only a victory to him. She had dared doubt his expertise with women, and he had wasted a few minutes removing that doubt.

"No, you get it, Mr. Belmont. I just quit," she said tonelessly.

"Nonsense. Hurry up. I'm expecting Hamilton's call any minute and I need that file."

"Call Mrs. Coyle. She's your secretary." Christina walked out the door and on through the reception room, looking neither left nor right. Distantly she heard his startled voice calling her name, but she ignored it. She was on the elevator, and then she was, astonishingly enough, parking her car in front of the boardinghouse without the slightest recollection of having driven there.

She had quit Belmont Enterprises. The thought kept stunning her, slamming her heart like a physical blow. Logic warred with feminine outrage as she climbed the three flights of stairs. No man could treat Christina Lacey like that, she firmly told herself. All the intolerable things she had put up with swarmed through her mind—his mocking taunts, his rudeness, his total lack of consideration, his dictatorial manner—*Do this, Miss Lacey, do that, Miss Lacey. My coffee, Miss Lacey!* How on earth had she put up with that despicable boor! Well, no more. She was free of Daniel Belmont. The telephone rang just as she stepped inside the door. Knowing in advance who it was, her voice was icy when she answered. "Miss Lacey speaking—"

"*Miss Lacey speaking* had better be back here at the office in ten minutes or *Miss Lacey speaking* will be *Miss Lacey screaming!*" Daniel roared.

"Your memory is faulty, Mr. Belmont. I just quit, remember?"

Christina slammed down the receiver—the nerve of the man! And right this second he was probably plowing through his hair with both hands and assigning her to wherever disloyal secretaries go. "Swine!" she muttered. A few more satisfying descriptives crossed her mind, but she was not in the habit of using them. A damn shame too, she thought. She would need boxes to pack . . .

Where was she going if she packed? Christina found herself standing at the window staring blindly down at the burly men loading a huge semi. When the telephone rang again, she nearly broke her neck getting to it. Greg Stafford's voice was a decided shock, but she heard herself agreeing to dinner with him that night.

Well, why not, she thought dully. She could pack tomorrow. The afternoon was lovely, and she decided to go to the beach.

Her mind barely registered the short trip to the shore. Keeping to the water's edge, Christina walked the length of silver sand, so deep in her bitter thoughts that the beauty around her made no impression. A deep sadness fought with the satisfaction of having shocked Daniel with her resignation. However much it pleased her ego, the ache in her heart was a very real pain.

Why had he kissed her like that? Because he couldn't resist a challenge? If so, how could she have responded so wantonly to a man who saw her only as a challenge? Christina had no answer for this smarting question either. Her emotions were a swirl of confusion and a nagging sense of guilt deepened it. She ought not to want his kisses, she ought not to long for those moments when he spoke gently and smiled warmly and looked at her softly. She ought not, Christina bleakly admitted, but she did.

She sat down on the sand and hugged her knees, staring at the water and seeing Daniel's face when he was off guard. She had sensed within him a great capacity for tenderness, yet rarely was he tender. Was he ashamed of it? She sat up with her next striking thought. Had he been deeply hurt by a woman and thus guarded his heart against a possible recurrence?

Christina slumped again. Daniel Belmont, assertive, self-assured, invincible. It seemed hardly likely, and at any rate, what did that have to do with the incident in his office?

An entire day spent in self-analysis resolved absolutely nothing. At sunset, feeling dispirited, she went home to dress for her dinner date.

The restaurant Greg chose was charmingly French, the food delicious, the lighting diffused and intimate, and she had never been so bored in her life. Greg was a peculiarly colorless man with sandy hair and neatly clipped mustache, and perhaps not so guileless as he seemed. Although his questions concerning her job were always light and casual, she belatedly realized that he extracted a lot of information, touching on the sensitive area of her relationship with Daniel so delicately that she found herself freely confiding her distaste for speculative gossip.

He listened quietly, then assured her that he understood her ticklish position; his trust in Christina Lacey was absolute. "I'm glad someone's is," she murmured dryly. Briefly, she was tempted to confide in him. But if she disclosed her resignation, she would have to explain why, and they really weren't that close. Yet she couldn't just up and leave town without some explanation. What to do?

"Excuse me?" a familiar voice interjected like a shock of ice water. Christina looked up into green eyes resembling chunks of granite. Hastily she withdrew her hand from Greg's, not even knowing how it got there.

"Good evening, Greg," Daniel said pleasantly before turning back to Christina. "Miss Lacey, you have succeeded in fouling up my entire schedule for this week, ruined my day, destroyed my dinner by tracking you down—I trust that's enough?" He glanced sharply at the hand that had unaccountably slid into Greg's again. "I will see you tomorrow morning at nine sharp. Is that clear? *Is* that clear, Miss Lacey?"

Impossibly, Christina heard herself saying, "Yes, Mr. Belmont."

"Very well. Good night, Greg—please excuse the intrusion. Miss Lacey," Daniel said, and left them.

"What the devil was that all about?" Greg asked, looking astonished.

Her eyes followed the tall imperious figure until it disappeared. "Oh, Greg . . . oh, good grief!" Feeling positively lightheaded with the sweetness of relief, Christina covered her face and helplessly began to laugh.

Chapter Five

"Did this just come in?" Daniel asked irritably.

"No, sir, it came in Tuesday," Christina replied.

"Why haven't I seen it?" he demanded.

"Because you were in London," she patiently explained. "I called and gave them your comments on the meeting. A Mr. Jakes called back. He says the design can be modified to meet the revised specifications, but it will be expensive. I included his conversation and the figures he named—"

"Where?" Daniel growled, rattling the papers in his hands. Repressing her annoyance, Christina walked behind him and leaned over his shoulder, flipping through the pages until she found the paper.

Daniel had been thoroughly disagreeable since her resignation and subsequent return. By tactical agreement, they had avoided the subject, but it crept into her mind with odd little tentacles of warmth, which she rather enjoyed. Two weeks had done nothing to mellow his mood. She stayed on her best efficient, impersonal secretary behavior, choking down hot retorts and the urge to violently disarrange that glossy cap of hair until she felt very near detonation point.

"The revised estimate is . . ." She ran a peach-tinted nail down the rows of figures. "Here—and this is the breakdown of individual costs."

Her hip rubbed his forearm as she explained. Unnerved by the contact, she carefully eased away, but she found his arm yet touching, as if it had somehow increased in width. When her voice faltered, he gave her a piercing upward glance.

"All right. I've got it. Drop this by Data Processing to be put into the computer," he ordered.

"Yes, sir," Christina cheerily replied. At times she still felt like a glorified office boy. Daniel seemed to take a perverse delight in sending her instead of one of the office girls. Ah, well, she thought with a philosophical shrug, that arrogant pride of his must demand some form of tribute, and apparently this was it.

When she reached for the document, Daniel retained possession. "On second thought, give it to Diana," he said. A host of differing expressions flitted across his face like a restless wind. A man at odds with himself, Christina reflected as she dropped the papers on the secretary's desk. His inner restiveness had been evident to her keen perception for weeks now.

Tucking her blouse into the waistband of her slim brown skirt, she gave herself a swift check in the mirror before stepping back inside his office. Flat green eyes raked her up and down as she closed his door and stood awaiting further orders. Further growls, she thought spitefully, but her face was serenely composed. Not for the world would she provoke him again!

He glanced in her direction, and she knew he had taken in every detail of her attire with that two-second perusal. Nervously she fingered the open collar of her cream silk blouse, wondering if anything was out of place as he gave her another oblique look.

"Miss Lacey, you said your parents were buried near Harlingen?"

"Why, yes," she replied, surprise escaping into her voice at this totally unrelated question.

"I'm sending the plane to Brownsville this afternoon to pick up some clients. If you'd like, I can send it earlier. Harlingen is very near Brownsville. It's eleven now—if you left immediately, you'd have ample time to . . . do whatever you liked and return at four with the plane."

Would he never cease to confound her? Christina was too delighted to react indifferently. "Oh, yes, Mr. Belmont!" Catching herself up short, she continued, "But that would mean an entire day lost from work, and we've such a backlog. How could you—that is, can we afford it?"

Daniel's smile sliced. "I think I can manage an entire day without you, Miss Lacey. I often got along fine before you joined the firm."

On fire with chagrin, Christina struggled with her temper. "Yes, of course," she replied. Clasping her hands behind her, she waited while he contacted the pilot and explained the change of schedule. It was an effort to contain her pleasure. She had not been back to the cemetery since the simple ceremony uniting her parents in death as they had been so beautifully united in life.

This sudden flash of consideration from her grizzly bear of a boss was baffling, but then, he was a baffling man, she reminded herself, smiling as he turned to her again.

"It's all arranged—Rodney says when you're ready," Daniel said, refering to the nice young pilot. "Please keep in mind, takeoff is at four, whether or not you're aboard the plane," he ended brusquely.

"Yes, sir. Thank you, Mr. Belmont," she replied, quietly sincere.

"You're welcome." Daniel stood up so swiftly, she stumbled back.

His mouth curled in a dour grin. "You need not cringe, Miss Lacey. I have no desire to molest you," he mocked.

Blushing, she stammered, "Y-Yes, sir—I mean no, sir." The dimple flashed like a neon sign, a revealing signal of the retort she chewed up and swallowed. She suddenly wondered if her un-flappable mask of cool indifference these past two weeks hadn't succeeded in pricking more than his ego.

The firm line of mouth held despite the twitch at the corners. Daniel moved to the tiny bar concealed in the floor-to-ceiling bookshelves and took out a heavy glass. Startled, Christina watched as he poured a shot of cognac and savored a sip. The blue-clad shoulders slumped just the smallest fraction as he looked at her with hooded sea-green eyes. This darkening of hue was quite as telling as her dimpling twist of mouth.

She tried to keep her gaze fixed on the window,

but it was impossible to ignore this contradiction to habit. "A drink—before noon?" she murmured.

Daniel's eyes flicked her like the tip of a lash. "It's my birthday, Miss Lacey. Cheers," he said grimly.

"I didn't know . . . how old are you, Mr. Belmont?" she asked, wincing at her artificially bright voice. Of course she knew, but she had to say something, and this was all that came to mind.

"Thirty-four, Miss Lacey—an ancient thirty-four," he mocked.

Christina stared at him. His dark hair was mussed as though by a breeze, and there was something amiss in the chill set of his features. He looked, of a sudden, like a vulnerable man, and she experienced a welling gush of tenderness.

"Not so ancient," she ruefully conceded. "Happy birthday." Acting purely on impulse, Christina walked over to him, placed her hands on his shoulders, rose up on tiptoe, and brushed a kiss on his mouth.

"Why, Miss Lacey! A milestone has been passed —you actually offered a kiss. But is that the best you can do?" he drawled, eyeing the wave of color staining her cheeks.

"Certainly not! But it's the best I want to do!" she flared.

"I'm trying to believe that," he assured.

Christina fell into the trap with ridiculous ease. She cupped his face and tried to kiss him, but the dark head refused to lower and she could barely reach his chin. "Well, bend down here, damn it!" she snapped.

"Yes, Miss Lacey," Daniel murmured.

The arms she expected to enfold her remained at

his side. Inflamed at this indifference to her offering, Christina stepped closer until her breasts pressed softly against his chest, her hands sliding through his hair, molding the shape of his head with caressing fingertips. She was swiftly losing the purpose of her kiss. The heady taste of his mouth unleashed a primitive desire that gathered force behind the restraints she had set for herself. As she heard his harsh intake of air and felt his arms wrap tightly around her, Christina knew a triumph as intoxicating as the kiss he rapidly took over.

Far too briefly, his mouth explored her inviting lips. Daniel raised his head. She looked up at him through her thick fringe of lashes, the gleam of violet eyes barely visible as her lips curved into a purely female smile. And then she was being kissed again with dizzying passion!

Roughly Daniel pulled her closer to the powerful maleness of his body. The sensuality of him raced hotly in her blood. Murmuring with delight, Christina wound her arms around him and kissed him with shameless ardor.

When he released her, Daniel smiled crookedly. "I thank you, Miss Lacey—that was very nice. You're coming along quite well. Well, the pilot is waiting," he reminded.

Fast regretting her unprofessional conduct, Christina rewarded him with a stony glare. "Thank *you*, Mr. Belmont—such a compliment scatters my senses," she tartly returned. "I hope the rest of your birthday is equally enjoyable."

"Oh, I'm quite certain it will be," Daniel said smoothly. "You did send the flowers I ordered for Miss Manning, did you not?"

Christina picked up her smart brown blazer. "Certainly. Have I ever failed you? Good-bye, Mr. Belmont."

"Good-bye, Miss Lacey. See you tomorrow."

"Don't remind me," she muttered, storming sedately toward the door.

"Miss Lacey?"

She stopped and warily turned to face him. "Yes, sir?"

"Thank you for the birthday present," Daniel said huskily.

For an instant she was puzzled, then Christina realized he was referring to her kiss. She looked at him searchingly, but no mockery stained his fine eyes.

"You're welcome," she said softly. Daniel smiled, then turned back to his desk.

"Miss Lacey?" His voice stopped her progress again. He grinned, the mischievous quirk of lips that never failed to quicken her heart. "Being thirty-four might not be half bad," he said thoughtfully.

Knowing she was probably cow-eyed with tenderness, Christina tried flippancy. "From where I stand, it doesn't *look* half bad. You're remarkably well preserved for a man of such antiquity."

"Humph!" Daniel picked up a folder and handed it to her. "Give this to Diana when you leave. Tell her I want it in triplicate, and if at all possible, without errors. Oh, and give Rodney a message for me. If you need an hour or so longer at the cemetery —" He shrugged expressively.

"Thank you, I appreciate that. Where are your parents buried?" she asked curiously.

"One here, one in California." He smiled wryly.

"A rather inconvenient arrangement. You run along now. I'll see you tomorrow."

"Yes. Tomorrow." They both smiled at the curious sweetness of the word. "Bye," Christina said, and left the office for the poignant pleasure this day would bring.

As she watched the city vanish behind a fluffy cloudbank, Christina shook her head in wonder at the man who had given it to her like an extravagant gift wrapped in newspaper. Would she ever really know Daniel Belmont? Her mouth curved in a soft smile. Did Daniel Belmont really know himself?

Becoming accustomed to the incredible heat of a Texas summer was a major accomplishment for Christina. "Ohio gets hot in July and August, but I rarely had the feeling I was walking through a sauna," she told Mrs. Coyle.

"Well, we have lovely falls, winters, and springs— three disagreeable months out of twelve isn't a bad ratio," Mrs. Coyle loyally declared. Remembering the length and severity of a midwestern winter, Christina had to agree with that.

September offered only moderate relief, but October was glorious. Autumn in Texas had a rare golden quality she found enchanting.

The only flaw in her enjoyment was the lack of someone to share her pleasure with, Christina reflected. She could just imagine Daniel's look if she began rhapsodizing about the weather! She felt so familiar with his reactions by now, she could imagine that arch of his eyebrow with flawless precision. Only this morning she had called his attention to the crisp good smells of an autumn morning, and what did it get her? A grunt and a sour look.

Christina flipped onto her back and floated, dreamily content in the nearly deserted pool. How very easy it was to become accustomed to luxury! Before she came to Texas, she had never stayed in a hotel, flown in a plane, known the wicked pleasure of ordering a meal without first checking prices. What a child that sad, forlorn Christina had been when Daniel had so providentially run into her, she mused. So raw and naive—like an unripened peach.

Not only an ignorant child, but a belligerent one, she confessed, recalling the night he had hired her. The memory still had the power to make her blush. Well, she was a much altered person now—sleek, poised, sophisticated, Christina assured herself. At least on the outside. Inside still had room for improvement. Climbing out of the pool, she wrapped herself in a velvety towel. She felt wonderfully refreshed by her swim, quite up to facing tonight's formal banquet. Taking off her cap and shaking out her hair, she walked at a brisk pace down the mottled brick path.

The city in which they were staying was as charming as a postcard—or as charming as she thought it might be, she amended. This was her third trip to San Antonio, and all she ever saw of it was the tantalizing view from a plane window.

When she opened the door to her room and stepped inside, Christina stopped with a gasp of surprise. A moss-lined wicker basket of orchids sat on the table. Her flaring excitement died at once; they were probably from Greg. The man acted like he owned her lately, and while he was pleasant company, he was nothing more than that.

But she had to admit his flowers were enchanting!

She touched one, and the luminous pink blossom swayed like an exotic butterfly on its long, arching stem. Picking up the card, she read it with a series of tingling shocks. How well she knew that bold, sprawling handwriting!

When she read it aloud, the shocks continued. "Happy anniversary, Miss Lacey. It's been an interesting six months. Daniel Belmont."

Overcome with delight, Christina dropped the towel on the thick beige carpet. Six months, she thought, turning on the bathwater. Six months of the most stimulating days of her life. She admitted it freely, she loved her job. Its unique flavor was sometimes bittersweet, but she lived in an atmosphere of sparkling excitement, and it was inconceivable that she could ever again exist in a nine-to-five clerical routine.

Stripping off her suit, she lowered herself into the perfumed water and let her mind drift back through the swift passage of time. Admittedly, although she still thrilled to her glittering lifestyle, it was the vibrantly attractive man who dominated her world that made it all so delightful. Their prickly relationship had changed very little. He was still the same sardonic, tyrannical, maddening man who could make her melt with a casual touch and smile with mocking amusement at her involuntary reaction.

She trod softly, only too aware how easily he could shatter her contrived indifference. Nonetheless, at times she still lost her temper and flew into him, provoking the dry response, "Miss Lacey, I am not in the mood for hissing kittens." The soft-shelled Christina had matured in other ways, too, she concluded with a sensual smile. If she was brave enough to challange, she was strong enough to accept the consequences. No one had ever made her so intensely aware of being a woman.

Even so, the pleasure she derived from being near him was utterly inexplicable, Christina confessed— since his manner toward her alternated between casual indifference and snappish impatience! Knowing she was a valuable addition to Belmont Enterprises helped her to control her anger.

She had even, although with more difficulty, accepted the slanted references to Daniel Belmont's "beautiful secretary." As she gained poise and a visible gloss of sophistication, the speculative wonder increased, swirling around her ears like the annoying buzz of mosquitoes. When they appeared together in public, she could not fault Daniel's behavior, nor lay any blame for conjecture on his shoulders, she thought proudly. The impression he managed to convey of complete immunity to Miss Lacey's charms was obscurely galling, but since it shielded her, she supposed she ought to appreciate it.

Despite Miss Manning's offhand announcement of their upcoming nuptials, she had not snared the city's "most eligible bachelor," and the coy hints she continued to drop to columnists and mutual friends alike were dispassionately shrugged off by the man she professed to love. Christina soon realized that no one made Daniel Belmont do anything he chose not to, and she could not help but feel a pang of pity for a woman reduced to this devious attempt to force his hand. Daniel still dated her, but Christina was no longer required to order flowers for Miss Manning. And judging from the look on his face, when Lisa's calls interrupted office routine, he was finding her a bit of a nuisance.

Granted, Christina's compassion was mixed with relief as a succession of other beauties were photographed hanging on to his tux sleeve like exotic flowers. There was safety in numbers. Safety for what, she preferred not to answer. Nor the reason for her bitter disappointment at realizing that Daniel regarded women as a collector's item, enjoyed and then discarded when they began to bore him.

A rippling shiver made Christina conscious of the unpleasantly cool bathwater, as well as the time she'd wasted daydreaming. After toweling and perfuming, she hurried to the closet. Even though she knew little about her employer's personal life, she did know that he liked glowing colors, especially the color red. The designer gown she unwrapped was a midsummer's dream in flame chiffon.

The halter-style bodice crisscrossed her breasts, becoming two softly draped straps that fastened around her neck, leaving her back enticingly bare to the waist. Happily she studied her radiant image. She would have Daniel all to herself tonight—he had made no date for this dinner. That he even required her presence tonight was explained with a curt, "This is not a social function, Miss Lacey. You are still on the job." She had not yet solved this pleasurable puzzle; Daniel got quite testy when she queried him on the subject. No matter. That he did want her there was enough for Christina, who could sometimes regress to adolescent simplicity, she cheerfully conceded.

The telephone pealed its imperious summons. Knowing who it was before she picked up the receiver, Christina hurried to answer it. Greg's bland voice rattled her badly. He was attending the banquet tonight and was looking forward to seeing her, he said, chuckling at her surprise.

Christina put him off with a vague reply, her mind churning as he went on and on. Greg had proposed to her last week, and he was becoming insistent upon an answer. Her protests that she did not love him were brushed aside as inconsequential; she would learn to care, and meantime he had enough love for the both of them.

When she had deliberately dropped Greg's proposal into casual conversation with Daniel, he reacted in typical Daniel fashion. "Well, I suppose he's a good catch. If you like, I'll look into his bank balance to ensure you're acting wisely," he drawled, smiling as if amused at her efforts to dismiss his cavalier attitude toward what she considered an honor.

The violet eyes showering sparks all over his face had provoked the usual warning, and she had come to her senses as he began moving toward her like a sleek jungle cat stalking its prey. Crossing swords with this man was dangerous, and she tried to avoid it if possible, but he was so infuriating!

And not at all jealous of Greg Stafford, she admitted with such desolation it shocked her. His spiteful taunts concerning her "boyfriend" were merely another way he derived enjoyment at her expense.

The telephone rang again as soon as she replaced the receiver. This time Daniel's brusque voice stabbed her ear. "Miss Lacey, would you come here—at once, please?" The sharp click as he hung up underscored her opinion of his lordly manner—if he'd requested that deep green chair to "come here at once," then he would expect it to do so without delay!

Resignedly Christina headed for the connecting door and rapped so sharply her knuckles stung. That she never locked it between them was an unconscious symbol of her trust in the man who slept just a wall away.

At his clipped command, she entered and closed the door behind her, feeling at once the irresistible pull of the tall figure standing with his back to her, a hand raking through his hair as he scrutinized a document. He was dressed in slacks, shoes, and a short white terry robe. His hair curled damply at his nape. Even from this distance she could smell the clean scent of his after-shave. He swung around. "Miss Lacey, do you—"

Christina had the sensation of being suspended between time and space as she stood under the spotlight of searching green eyes. His face intense, Daniel stared at her for a moment of unguarded emotion. "Miss Lacey, you are lovely," he said in a surprisingly unsteady voice.

The odd intensity of his gaze, the thrill of his undisciplined words held her rooted to the spot. His loosely belted robe revealed the strong thrust of his throat and V-shaped line of tanned skin furred with curly dark hair. Her heart hammering, Christina lifted her chin in proud defiance. She had not yet gotten around to styling her hair, and the heavy black satin mass swayed on her shoulders.

"Come here," Daniel said huskily.

Christina floated across the room with fluid grace, hearing the whisper of her gown with each step. "Turn around, slowly," he softly instructed. Lifting her arms above her head, she performed a slow, tantalizing piroutte and came to rest facing him again. Was he going to kiss her? She was aching for it, and ashamed of that, but it had been so long since she'd felt his arms around her! Daniel circled her in silent appraisal while she stood immobile, a glowing column of flame incapable of resistance.

She felt the soft touch of his lips on her shoulder as a tongue of fire. "What is that perfume you're wearing?" he asked so low she strained to hear his words. Daniel turned her around and stood studying her for a moment. "Well, you pass inspection," he said with his usual sardonic smile, but it didn't quite come off this time.

"I'm delighted you approve," she said dryly. "Oh, thank you for the orchids—they're exquisite."

"No thanks required—I find such small gestures usually pay rich dividends with women . . . or employees." His smile was only inches from her face, and the hooded green eyes gleamed between their sheltering lashes.

"Yes, I suppose they do. But they're enchantingly beautiful and I was . . . Why did you have to spoil it?" she asked in a half whisper. They no longer seemed quite so beautiful.

Daniel looked uncomfortable. "I didn't mean to spoil it, Miss Lacey. I selected them myself," he said quietly. "I don't normally send such exotic flowers to my secretaries—or anyone else."

"Then I shan't throw them into the trash can after all," she said. He laughed. Helplessly she swayed toward him—and then she was in his arms, caught tightly close as his mouth met hers with an urgency that could melt bones. Her hands slid up his chest to the parting of his robe, and then beneath it, spreading out over his satin-smooth shoulders as his fiercely possessive kiss burned her lips.

"Christina, Christina!" he muttered feverishly as his hands glided caressingly down her naked back—down, down, hard and warm and greedy for the soft mounds tantalizing his fingers. Hazily aware of this intimate touch, Christina was yet caught up in a swirl of rapturous excitement. The glory of being in his arms, crushed against his inflexible strength, and kissed with breathtaking passion drove all thought from her mind.

Her head arched back as his mouth brushed a teasing trail of kisses down her neck to her throat. The jarring shock of her lips on his chest, deliciously spicy and warm as she pressed tiny kisses all the way up to his ear, weakened her knees until she was held erect only by the arms around her. When her small teeth gently bit into his earlobe, he responded with a gasp. His arms tightened around her. The blaze of erotic pleasure went on and on as he kissed her. She could not—would not—heed the warning signals clamoring deep in her hazed mind. Lost in a cloud of tumultuous sensation, Christina was conscious only of this incandescent flame engulfing her entire being. The bliss of knowing his excitement was tinder for her own. Stretching upward, she thrust her hands through his hair and pulled his mouth to hers with a wildness that shocked some remote part of Christina Lacey.

"Darling, my darling," Daniel whispered. The words sang in her mind and tumbled against the lips he kissed so hungrily.

Daniel set her from him with stunning abruptness. Dazed, breathing with soft little gasps, Christina could only stare at him in wide-eyed confusion. He turned sharply and strode to the window. As though struggling with his own demons, Daniel stood rigidly silent while she sagged against the table like a rag doll.

Why had he stopped? He must have known she was beyond resistance and yet he had set her from him with rough hands. Shame, deep and merciless, poured through her. She had responded with wanton ardor—again!

When he approached her, the familiar sardonic glint lit his eyes. "Miss Lacey, you're much improved," he said lightly. "Even to the point of stirring a man . . ." His smile thinned as he gathered a handful of silken curls. "Have you been practicing? With Greg, perhaps?"

It was a vicious jibe. Jerking his hand away from her hair, she turned and opened the door. "Running away, Miss Lacey?" he taunted.

Christina was nearly incoherent with hurt and anger. Her hair flying about her face, she wheeled in icy bravado. "You are without doubt the most despicable man I have ever met!" she spat.

"I'll pick you up in twenty minutes, Miss Lacey," he absently replied.

Incapable of speaking, Christina slammed the door with a resounding bang. His orchids glowed pink in the lamplight of her room. She ached to destroy them, but she could not. She raged around the lovely room in passionate need to relieve the tension built up inside of her. Damn him!

"Oh, cool it, Christina," she acidly advised herself. "So you got kissed—so what? And it was you who started it, remember?"

Pride banished guilt and hurt and whatever else she felt. When a hard-knuckled rap sounded on her door precisely twenty minutes later, she walked over and calmly opened it.

"I trust you're ready, Miss Lacey?" asked Daniel, cocking an eyebrow.

Another irritation, she thought furiously. After months of acquaintance, this formal address was ridiculous. But she knew as well as she knew her name that if *she* suggested a change, he would remind her who set policies in *his* organization.

"As you can see, I'm quite ready," she smoothly replied.

Daniel smiled and gently touched her hair. "Yes, you are—and you look lovely, Miss Lacey," he assured. And her heart started singing again.

Chapter Six

How could he do this to her? Christina wondered incredulously. How could he arouse the desire to brush that lock of hair obscuring one eyebrow? How could she want so desperately to cradle his face in her hands and kiss that insouciant smile? She wanted to kill him!

Utterly baffled by the force of her emotions, she said warningly, "Mr. Belmont—"

"I suggest you compose yourself. There will be photographers," he murmured. Taking her arm with a proprietary air, Daniel escorted her to the elevator.

She would kill him! Even as her heart quivered with outrage, Christina fought against the maddening pull of devastatingly attractive male. His midnight blue tuxedo and white shirt were appallingly effective. She scowled so ferociously that he threw back his head and laughed.

"Oh, Miss Lacey, what would I do without your temper tantrums to spice up my dull life!" he crooned. Green eyes danced wickedly as her scowl enveloped her entire face. Incredibly enough, she felt an outrageous urge to laugh with him.

To her dismay, she was seated beside Greg Stafford. Daniel greeted him, smiled at Christina, and walked from the room. Fifteen minutes later he returned with a stunning brunette whose topaz eyes dismissed Christina immediately after the brief introduction.

Eyeing the broad back Daniel turned to her, Christina clenched her fists as his indulgent laugh mingled with the woman's velvety voice. He had said nothing about a dinner companion, leading her to believe that they would spend the evening together.

Daniel suddenly turned and leaned to her ear. "Miss Lacey, why am I being stabbed in the back?" he asked resignedly.

"If only I had a knife!"

"Tut-tut. May I remind you, people are watching," he murmured with a charismatic smile.

Christina's quick glance around confirmed his claim. She composed her face and said through clenched teeth, "Yes, Mr. Belmont."

"Now do mind your manners—and pay some attention to Greg, hm? He looks woefully neglected," Daniel blandly suggested.

It was all she could do not to slap him. That he had given her into Greg's custody for the evening choked her with fury. The high-handed, self-centered, ill-mannered *barbarian!* And that this one man had the power to raise her blood to boiling point!

Daniel was watching. "Enjoy yourself, Miss

Lacey," he murmured before shifting to greet some-one.

Prior to tonight he had not touched her in weeks. He regarded with amused indulgence Greg's light kiss of greeting. And if there was a man she detested any more than Daniel Belmont, she had yet to meet him, Christina firmly decided.

Time assumed the creeping quality of cold molasses. As soon as decently possible, Christina suggested a breath of fresh air, and Greg readily consented. He was certainly feeling his drinks tonight, she reflected as they wandered through the moonlit grounds. Undeterred by her silence, he kept up a steady stream of chatter.

The breeze caressing her flushed skin felt marvelously cool and restoring. Christina lifted her face to enjoy it—and found herself being kissed in a most unpleasant fashion! Reflexively, her flat palm connected with his cheek in a shockingly loud slap. Appalled at having actually struck someone, Christina wrenched free of his embrace and hurried down the path to the hotel.

She was nearly running when Daniel strode around the corner. Just barely avoiding a collision by his quick step aside, he caught and steadied her, his voice low and sharp. "What's the matter, Christina?"

She snatched a steadying breath. "Nothing, I was just taking a breath of air, that's all. I think I'll go to my room now—"

Catching sight of Greg, Daniel glanced at her flushed face and dropped his hands. "But of course. Sleep well, Miss Lacey."

The faint contempt in his voice widened her eyes. "Good night," she said tersely. Christina hurried around him and continued on to the elevator with rigid control. All her anger had faded, and its replacement was raw pain.

The tranquillity of her room was priceless. As she closed the door, Christina began to shake, whether from her own turmoil or the cool air of the room she wasn't sure. She wrapped her arms around herself and leaned back against the solid surface. A knock on the other side jolted her heart. She opened it, then shrank in dismay at sight of Greg's florid face.

"What do you want, Greg?" she coolly inquired.

"You think I'm a fool, don't you, Christina—a gullible fool who will believe any fairy tale you care to spin!" came his astounding reply.

"Greg, I don't understand—"

Greg shoved his way inside and slammed the door behind him. "Oh, you understand, all right," he grated. "Daniel Belmont's *mistress!*"

Christina sagged against the door in sickened dismay. "Oh, Greg. You're wrong, very wrong," she said tiredly.

"You little liar!" Greg bit off. He grabbed her shoulders and shook her, his voice ringing in her ears with furious accusations.

Christina's shocked cry was silenced by a hard, punishing kiss. Shuddering with revulsion, she struggled wildly with the overwrought man. Dimly she heard Daniel enter his room, and this destroyed any urge to scream. How would he react to this? An embarrassing scene was the last thing she wanted! Yet Greg's embrace grew painfully tight. Despite her efforts to remain silent, Christina's protests increased until she let out a muffled scream.

A sharp rap on the connecting door was followed

by Daniel's voice. "Miss Lacey? Are you all right?" he called, knocking again.

Greg was too engrossed in what he was doing to heed the rising note of concern. Only when the door burst open and Daniel bounded into the room did he raise his head from Christina's. There was a moment of suspenseful silence. Maintaining his clasp around her, Greg looked at Daniel in icy challenge.

Christina felt torn in too many directions to do more than stare dumbly from one man to the other. Suddenly conscious of her disheveled appearance, her hands flew to her hair, making frantic attempts to smooth it. Why didn't someone say something! She could think of nothing sensible—not with those chill green eyes fixed on her face!

Daniel stood rigid as he assessed the situation. His hand gripped the doorknob. "Excuse me, Miss Lacey, I heard the sounds you were making and mistook them for . . . something else. My apologies, Greg," he drawled. Wheeling around, he stepped back through the door and closed it sharply.

Christina flung her hands against Greg's shoulders. "Get out of here, Greg—please, just get out of here," she cried wretchedly. The contempt in Daniel's eyes was acid in her heart.

A look of miserable confusion came over Greg's face. "Oh, Christina, I . . . all right," he muttered defeatedly. He walked out the exterior door.

Shaking with reaction, Christina collapsed on the couch. She felt Daniel's presence through the thin walls and she yearned mightily to go to him, to seek the comfort of his arms, to be held close and kissed gently, tenderly.

So great was her tormenting need, she was already

on her feet moving toward the connecting door when she caught herself. One glimpse in the mirror was enough to remind her she could not possibly confront Daniel looking like this. Her pale, tear-streaked face and wildly tumbled hair mocked her much worse than he had ever done. She dropped her face into her hands and cried without restraint.

Greg's perplexing accusation went round and round in her mind. Anxiously she examined the evening, but nothing untoward had happened that she could recall. Daniel had practically ignored her and she had reacted in kind.

Abruptly she dismissed it—Greg's opinion of her was of no significance. But Daniel's was a far different matter. She knew he thought he'd interrupted them and she must, for her own self-respect if nothing else, set straight his misconception.

Christina washed her face and restored her hair. Then, with considerable trepidation, she knocked on Daniel's door. When he curtly bid her enter, she stepped into his room, her eyes flying at once to his face.

As she struggled to steady her voice, his gaze sharpened with impatience. "Yes, Miss Lacey?"

"Mr. Belmont, please, you must—I want you to . . ." she began, but lost her courage.

A cruel smile thinned his mouth. "Miss Lacey, surely not two men in one night? Is Greg no longer *adequate?*" he asked, savagely humorous.

Christina gasped at his crudeness. "Please, I want to explain what you saw—"

"It was self-explanatory, believe me, Miss Lacey." He bit off her name with a snap of teeth. Making a visible effort to bring back his cynical smile, Daniel shook his head. "It surprised me, I admit. Here I took you seriously when you assured me you would never . . . well, not for pleasure, anyway. Maybe for something more solid."

His musing contempt evoked a hurt little cry from Christina. "No! It wasn't what you thought! He followed me to my room and forced his way in and—and attacked me—I swear it!"

A murderous look leapt to Daniel's eyes. "Attacked you?" he echoed very softly.

Christina's hands fluttered in confusion. "I don't mean—*attacked* me. I meant— He just came in, you see. I didn't invite him."

Daniel released a hissing breath. "From what I saw he didn't have to wait for an invitation," came his cynical reply.

"Isn't there a chance that what you saw might be misleading?"

"Perhaps. But you did go for a nice long walk in the moonlight, didn't you. And as for his using force, remember, I was right next door, and I heard no screams at all . . . quite the contrary," he drawled.

"That's not true and you know it! You heard the sounds I was making, you came rushing to my room—"

Daniel caught her arms. "The only sounds I heard were sounds of pleasure!" he gritted. "I know what I saw—you've entertained him before, haven't you, Miss Lacey!" His fingers dug into the soft flesh of her arms.

"N-no, I—Daniel, you're hurting me!" Christina cried.

"Tears," he accused bitterly. "Those beautiful eyes filling with tears—*damn* you, Christina!" He swept her into his arms and kissed her. Helplessly responsive, Christina returned his bruising kiss with all the love she felt for this perplexing man!

Daniel thrust her from him with a muttered curse. Her eyes huge and imploring, Christina shamelessly clung to him. "Daniel, please, please!" she pleaded without knowing exactly what she pleaded for.

Daniel looked down into her wet face. "I'd like you to go, please. I'm extremely tired and in no mood for this tonight." His teeth flashed stark white against his tanned skin. "Another time, perhaps," he said carelessly, and removed her hands from his shoulders.

Christina was flayed raw by his words. She loved him. As simply as flowers in spring, she loved him, deeply, hurtingly, irrevocably. The stunning realization drained her of everything but the numbed exhaustion seeping into her very bones. Childishly wiping her tears, she slowly raised her gaze to his face and received another shock. The mask which was second nature to this man had suddenly cracked, and he looked painfully young and vulnerable, his dark eyes touchingly naked without that sardonic gleam to shield them. Recognizing a Daniel Belmont as defenseless to pain as any man, her heart swelled with love. She stepped toward him with only one purpose in mind—to hold him, to cradle him close and comfort him. To give him back the strength she knew he must have to be the man she loved above all others, Christina thought fiercely.

Before she had completed a step, Daniel recovered. The familiar mockery fired his eyes as he cocked his head and laughed. "Miss Lacey, must I throw you out bodily, hm?"

Her hands dropped to her sides. She must have imagined it, Christina thought tiredly. "No, that won't be necessary. I'm tired too, so I'll go quietly," she said with a ghost of a smile.

His mouth twisted into something resembling a grin. "I imagine you are tired," he silkily agreed. "Vigorous exercise can be exhausting."

"I told you the truth," she said with returning spirit. "Greg Stafford has never done more than kiss me—and certainly not what you're implying. If you choose not to believe me, then I—"

"Miss Lacey, what you do in your free time is your concern, not mine," Daniel cut in. His eyes were as cold and indifferent as the deep green core of an arctic glacier.

"My sentiments exactly," Christina stated. There was nothing more to say, and even if there had been, she was too near tears to risk it. She nodded and turned to leave.

"Sleep well, Miss Lacey."

The soft, mocking voice lashed her like a whip. Christina closed the door between them, and this time she locked it.

When sunshine roused her to morning, Christina sat up in bed rubbing her eyes, wondering why she had awakened feeling so weary—and then the recollection of the night before crashed down upon her like icy water! Flinging back the coverlet, she swung her legs to the floor and massaged her shoulders.

The mirror revealed the price of her night of weeping. After a single glance at her white face and puffy eyelids, she walked on to the bathroom. A hot shower, followed by an icy rinse, restored a modicum of energy to her aching body. She must have tossed and turned all night to be this sore, Christina reflected; there were no marks on her ivory skin, but she felt bruised all over.

As she dried off, she gave herself firm orders. She would think no more about last night. Enough time had been spent analyzing every single moment. If Daniel did not bring it up, it would not be mentioned. They must bury it if she was to continue working for him—and she could not give that up! A life that did not include the sight of his beloved face was utterly inconceivable.

"You must be mad, Christina," she muttered, recalling that "beloved face" last night. Mad or not, she had to face the fact that her day did not begin until Daniel Belmont looked at her and said, "Good morning, Miss Lacey," no matter *how* he said it. She must not betray the slightest sign of her foolish love. He would find it terribly amusing—she was quite sure of that.

Since they were flying home today, she dressed for her own pleasure, choosing a rose-sprigged dimity frock with a full skirt and an apple green sash to define her trim waist. She gathered her hair at the back of her neck and tied it with a green velvet ribbon, then put on strappy white sandals. As she anxiously examined her reflection, a warm smile curved her lips. She looked exactly as she hoped— appealingly young and innocent. It would be her only defense against Daniel's waspish tongue.

It was nine o'clock when he summoned her. She drew a deep breath and opened the door. His living room was scattered with newspapers and several coffee cups sat on various tables. Evidently Daniel hadn't slept very well last night either; although his face appeared tired and drained, he seemed immaculate as ever in a blue chambray shirt and gabardine slacks. She had heard him go out last night, and it had been after three when he returned. But she did not care to speculate on his whereabouts.

He looked distinctly unfriendly when he finally raised his head to acknowledge her presence. "Good morning, Miss Lacey. I trust you slept well?" he asked sourly.

"Good morning. Yes, I slept fine."

Daniel grunted. His eyes flickered over her dress and moved on to the wall behind her, then wandered back in impassive appraisal. "Are you working today or going dancing?" Not waiting for her response, he continued, "I've ordered breakfast sent up. We'll go over these notes before we leave. . . . Your telephone is ringing," he pointed out on the third peal.

"I'm sure it's nothing important," Christina said evenly. She had no desire to provoke him. Daniel's manner had a menacing air this morning.

His smile was slow and dangerous. "Come now, Miss Lacey. Don't let a minor thing like business interfere with your love life," he said so cuttingly she decided to break the rules she had made.

"Mr. Belmont, do you wish to discuss last night so we can stop this silly sparring?" she asked calmly.

A white look of anger washed across his face. "I do not wish to discuss anything with you. I'm not the least interested in last night! What I would like to do is get to work. Do you think we can manage that?"

Her face paled at his sarcasm. The pain in her heart nearly shattered her composure. He looked so *hostile,* she thought, wretchedly close to tears. To gain time she began picking up papers. From under her lashes she noted his closed face, the glacial frost of green eyes watching her graceful movements. Forboding swamped her. They could not work in such an atmosphere—the tension between them was thick enough to slice!

To her vast relief, Daniel reverted to perfunctory professionalism as they concentrated on business. At noon he stood up and stretched with catlike suppleness. "Well, it's noon and I've a luncheon engagement. By the way, I wish to apologize for my behavior last night and my sharpness this morning. I admit I was way out of line, Miss Lacey," he said with an apologetic smile she instantly distrusted.

"I accept your apology, on the condition that you believe me," Christina coldly replied.

"Of course," he said, looking surprised. "I thought that was understood."

Christina opened her mouth, shut it, cleared her throat of wrathful words and said, "Very well. What is my schedule for this afternoon?"

"The rest of the day is yours. I've ordered a car and driver for you, and you're free to explore the city until six o'clock. We'll be leaving at six thirty. Enjoy yourself," he said, smiling with his offhand gift.

Christina's foolish, impractical heart melted, of course. A tiny smile dimpled one cheek—love made a person crazy at best. "Thank you, Mr. Belmont, you too."

"Well, I shall certainly try," Daniel assured. "Now go have fun, Miss Lacey. That's an order."

An ambiguous one, Christina thought, but she tried to obey it. She barely made it back to the hotel before six o'clock. Immediately it began to pour rain and she thought Daniel's call informing her that takeoff would be delayed was really quite unnecessary. Rain pounded her windows, and it was ominously black outside.

Around eight Daniel called again, and his voice cut through her loneliness as easily as a warm knife through butter. "I've decided we'll delay until morning. Good night, Miss Lacey."

"Good night, Mr. Belmont," she replied, her voice unsteady.

"You're not afraid of storms, are you?" he asked sharply.

"Ah, no, I find them exciting—when I'm not up there in them."

He chuckled. "Well, this one you can enjoy from your hotel room."

Christina hung up with a keen sense of loss. Knowing full well that nothing but Daniel's arms would warm her, she ran a hot bath to banish her inner chill.

The water grew tepid and she felt no better. To love someone so much you were stripped of natural pride and wanted only to give to him was a devastating admission. And there's no way you can change it, she thought bleakly. Desired or not, love was there, almost tangible in its power. Wrapping up in a towel, Christina opened her suitcase and extracted a satin dressing gown the color of the wild blue columbines that once grew in the woods behind her grandmother's house. In spring, she remembered, they carpeted the dappled glens and she would pick them, sky blue flowers wilting in a grubby little fist as a love offering. To paraphrase Daniel, that was a long time ago.

Absently she tied the velvet ribbons beneath her breasts. The wide, elasticized neckline framed her creamy shoulders and enticingly displayed the soft swells of her breasts. Wispy little curls feathered round her face beguilingly, but Christina was totally oblivious to her appeal.

Restlessly she roamed the dimly lit room. When someone knocked on the door, her heart jerked with apprehension. She opened it, but left the chain guard on; Greg's anxious face was the last thing in the world she wanted to see!

He was abjectly apologetic and humble. Christina felt nothing but annoyance at his plea of wine-fogged conclusions, insufferable jealousy, and agonizing regret. He begged her forgiveness and took forever doing it.

"It's all right, Greg," she said wearily. Despite her annoyance, she was not capable of outright cruelty. Everyone does things they later regret, she thought bitterly. Bidding him a gentle good night, she locked her door again. Greg's plea had stated that love separated a person from logic; he was absolutely right.

A few minutes later, the much sharper rap jerked her heart in a different way. Christina flung it open without reservation. She knew that knock and the hand that made it!

His jacket slung over one shoulder, Daniel lounged against the door frame in a pose of nonchalance. Raindrops glistened on his glossy hair and he smelled fresh and outdoorsy. Christina went weak with longing. "Good evening, Mr. Belmont," she said, clearing her throat.

"Miss Lacey. May I come in?" he asked, doing so.

"Were you out in this storm?" she asked, her eyes following the tall, slim figure filling her room with the warmth of a thousand suns. Fleetingly she wondered if he'd seen Greg leaving her room. She fervently hoped not.

Daniel threw his jacket over the back of a chair. "Yes, I was out—nasty, wasn't it. Have you eaten?"

"Yes, I had something sent up," she said. The vague wave of hand set the butterfly sleeve in motion. Daniel glanced down the shimmering gown.

"You look very nice," he said shortly.

Murmuring an inaudible thanks, Christina sat down on the couch and crossed her legs. The restless movement of the toe of a silver slipper peeping from the hem of her gown betrayed an inner turmoil as she watched him prowl around her room like a caged animal. The blue, shadow-striped shirt and fitted gray slacks he wore emphasized his powerful physique. When that beguiling lock of hair fell over his brow, she had to clasp her fingers tightly in her lap.

Daniel stopped in front of the couch to regard her with a look she could not fathom. "Ah, Miss Lacey," he sighed. When he stretched out his hands, she took them without thinking, and he drew her to her feet. Dark green eyes hungrily caressed her face and trailed down to the creamy swells of her breasts.

"Was your face unchanged after the accident?" he asked tightly. A long finger touched her nose and traced the delicate line of her jaw.

Startled, Christina said, "Yes, everything's the same."

The seductive finger trailed over her eyebrows, then traced the curve of her tremulous mouth as though setting it to memory by touch alone. "Little Miss Lacey," he said huskily. Daniel leaned down and kissed the pulsing hollow of her throat.

Christina stood rigid, her hands clenched at her side, trembling inside with the need to reach out and hold him! Little scraps of warning danced through her head, but they scattered too quickly to form a distinct command. Just maintaining this outward indifference required tremendous willpower, and she could not form the words that would send him away.

As if sensing this, Daniel cradled her face and kissed the tip of her nose before drawing back to smile into her eyes. "I prefer your hair down," he huskily chided, releasing it from its pins. She knew what was coming and she must stop it now—*now*, before she was stripped of all resistance, Christina desperately warned her yearning self. This was nothing more than expert tactics from what could only be called an expert.

His gaze was hypnotic. She could not unlock her eyes from his. Her thoughts would not connect.

As the silken mass of curls came tumbling down around his wrists, Daniel threaded both hands into it and lowered his face to hers. His mouth gently brushed hers, then moved over her face with lingering, feather-light kisses. Christina stood stiffly, a statue in his arms.

The lovely little kisses outlined the contours of her shoulders and the slender column of her neck, tantalizing, intoxicating whispers of warmth imprinted on her naked skin. Desperately Christina sought to resist the flash flood of desire welling up. To submit to his kisses was humiliation enough. To respond was a betrayal. But she wanted to love him, and she ached to hold him! The undercurrent of tension, always there, ready to come alive and

113

explode into blazing sparks of excitement, seemed to emanate from his body and whisper to hers of a rapture beyond her realm of experience.

His breath on her face was a caress, the smoldering gleam in his eyes a sensuous command. Christina resisted that command so weakly she made a tiny sound of protest. But he was too knowledgeable of the woman who watched him with wide violet eyes.

"Put your arms around me, Christina," he whispered seductively.

"No . . . I want you to go." Christina dredged the words from her last shreds of pride. She pulled free and backed away until the edge of the bed touched the backs of her knees.

Daniel followed, his hands hungrily reaching, gathering her into his arms. "No, you don't want me to go. I want you, my sweet Miss Lacey—I've always wanted you," he whispered on her mouth.

How could any woman resist him! Christina swayed into him as the last of her strength flowed from her bones and left only fluid behind. She wound her arms around him and held him tightly, fusing with him in a deep, passionate kiss. "Yes . . . oh, *yes!*" Daniel muttered thickly.

Somewhere she heard the wind crying like a desolate child. Somewhere music murmured and an inner voice chimed in unceasing alarm. But that was somewhere, and this was the breathtaking magic of hard, strong arms around her and thrilling closeness with the man she loved above everything and everyone!

Chapter Seven

Christina lost all contact with reality. There was nothing in her conscious world but this blue-flamed excitement wrapped in all-consuming love. It felt so beautifully right and natural to feel his hands on her body. The interplay of mouths and tongues pleasured her deeply as his kisses grew more frenzied. When he pushed down the neckline of her gown and curved his fingers around her breasts, she made only a small, weak sound of protest, which he took into his kiss.

Christina sank down on the bed with him. She was hazily aware of that voice crying *Danger!* in some remote section of her mind. But his hands were tenderly exploring, and he kissed her deeply as she turned into the aroused body fitting to hers.

Shocked by an intimate caress, she caught his hand, but his passion-slurred voice stayed her fingers. "Hold me, Christina. Hold me, sweetheart," he whispered. The beautiful endearment had a stunning effect on her senses, banishing resistance as nothing else could have done. Her arms wound around him in ardent compliance.

Slowly, so slowly, he turned her onto her back. His mouth dipped to her throat, the rough, moist rasp of his tongue sliding downward, pausing to torment and savor, moving again. And then she felt the hotness of it on her naked breasts, and she was sinking into a silken sea of desire.

Christina knew it was madness, but she also knew it was too late to stop now. Kisses would not satisfy their primitive hunger. She didn't *want* to stop him. To thrust aside the deliciously hard, warm body coming urgently to hers was far greater madness than their velvety lovemaking. The taut arousal of his thighs pressed insistently, needfully, his eyes shining deep into the hazed purple gaze fluttering open in soft surrender. Her hair spread a sheet of shimmering black satin across the pillow. Daniel ran his fingers through it, buried his face in it, whispered in it, "God, you are lovely, my Christina . . . so temptingly soft and lovely . . ." His eyes sought her face again, and she was drowning in them, drifting deep into the shining green and endless depths of them.

Christina felt a great surge of love for him and the need to express it was aching torment. The thrilling power of him, the sheer male strength straining against her softness, told her without words that the same fevered longing throbbed in his blood, yet he restrained himself to tenderness. And when tenderness gave way to mounting passion, when he kissed her love-sweetened lips as if he could not get enough of them, his roughening caresses betraying his male urgency, her own excitement increased. His tongue plunged deeply, in a sensuous rhythm his body strained to emulate. Mindlessly she pulled him closer until they lay enfolded in a perfection of dovetailing contours.

"Christina!" he muttered thickly.

Christina stilled at the raw, impassioned sound. Her eyes fluttered open in a searching look, and she made a small, wordless moan at what she saw. His face was starkly intense, his eyes glazed with passion. Just passion, just the urgency of a man's basic need for a woman, she thought bleakly. Primitive masculine lust. She turned her face aside as reality seeped into the rapturous glow of love. This meant nothing but temporary gratification to Daniel; it meant everything to her. She could not even contemplate what came afterward when he went his careless way and she was left with . . . what? A self-disgust so acrid she could taste it!

His mouth tugged at the corner of her lips, sweetly urgent, as demanding as the body pressing her down in arrogant male possession.

"No!" she said fiercely, pushing at his shoulders.

His face whitened. "No?" His kiss crushed her lips against her teeth before he raised his head to stare at her, his mouth a hard, thin line. "Stafford, but not me, Miss Lacey?" he asked in a soft, savage snarl.

"No! Not Greg—oh, please, Daniel!" Christina cried, aghast at his furious reaction.

He laughed, a contemptuous sound. "I met Greg in the hall, Miss Lacey. I'm pretty good at judging the quality of a man's smile, particularly when he's just left a woman," he said so viciously that Christina reeled.

Daniel flung himself off the bed, his eyes charring her with that icy contempt. "While I don't ordinarily get overwrought when a woman changes her mind, I do most bitterly resent being taken for a fool, Miss Lacey!" he gritted. Grabbing his jacket, he strode out of the door and slammed it behind him.

Christina got off the bed and shed her rumpled gown. She felt very strange, as if a vital nerve had been severed and left her utterly devoid of thought or emotion. And tired—tired to death. Moving with robot precision, she turned back the covers and snapped out the light.

It had been a traumatic day, and she just wanted to end it by going to sleep.

Despite her landlady's warning, when Christina stepped inside her own apartment next morning, she was overwhelmed by the masses of roses. All from Greg and all containing the same message; he was dreadfully sorry and he must see her again.

Christina dropped the cards into a wastebasket, opened a window to air the room, and listlessly unpacked her bags. Although she had blanked out all thoughts of the past two days, her spirits remained low. Daniel had not returned on the plane and his whereabouts were unknown to her. She had been relieved to postpone what could only be an embarrassing confrontation. She had the weekend to put things in proper perspective, and meanwhile it was good to be back in these homey surroundings.

When the telephone rang, she tensed, torn between dread and hope. It was the receptionist down

118

the hall. The two women had formed a casual friendship and Christina accepted without hesitation an invitation to spend the weekend at a beach house on nearby Padre Island.

Swimming, sailing, easy companionship—just the ticket, Christina thought grimly. Vowing to swim and sail and talk herself into exhaustion, she repacked her overnight bag.

The sea, the wind, the repeated dunkings in warm, choppy water were marvelous restoratives. Given a respite from brooding, and two nights of sleep so deep and dreamless they were just short of oblivion, Christina awoke Monday morning feeling reasonably cheerful. The day was likely to be unpleasant, she reflected as she dressed for work, but she felt confident of facing it with equanimity. What had seemed catastrophic in the dark of night had leveled off to simply an awkward situation that could be handled in an adult manner.

A thwarted attempt at seduction, nothing else, she told herself. Although why Daniel had reacted so violently to her decision to call if off was a puzzle she simply could not unravel. Since it was inconceivable that he felt jealous of Greg Stafford, she put it down to a badly scratched male ego.

The only thing that could not be put in its place was the memory of a thick, husky voice calling her sweetheart and darling. The endearments glowed like spots of sunshine at the back of her mind, impervious to scorn or logic.

Setting her shoulders, Christina gave her attention to the mirror again. "You will be calm, cool, and collected," she admonished the big, apprehensive eyes. "Businesslike, unemotional . . ." Her voice trailed off. No use borrowing trouble, Aunt Pauline always said. She would handle this as one handled any difficult situation—one step at a time.

Christina glanced at the overblown roses as she walked out the door. As for Greg Stafford, she would have to find some way to deal with the man. But not now. Confronting Daniel Belmont was enough to occupy her mind.

He wouldn't be in until noon, Mrs. Coyle informed her. With a noncommittal smile Christina strolled past the curious brown gaze and entered Daniel's office with a sense of coming home. The room was permeated with his presence, whether or not he was in it. She touched the tiny sculpture, then left his office for her own.

It was nearly twelve when her beloved tormentor requested her presence. Placing a hand on the doorknob, Christina paused to collect herself for a vitally needed moment. Butterflies swarmed in her stomach and her knees felt appallingly weak. "Enough, Christina," she scolded. Tapping lightly, she entered at his terse command.

"Good morning, Mr. Belmont," she greeted him, her heart hammering wildly and the butterflies going insane. Just seeing him sitting behind his desk, his head bent over his infernal papers, sent her pulse skyrocketing. She leaned against the door, suddenly fearful that her legs would carry her no farther. He wore a deep blue shirt with his gray suit, and his crisp, springy hair glistened with health.

His manner was neither uneasy, nor welcoming. Opaque green eyes surveyed her from head to toe. "Good morning, Miss Lacey. Did you have a pleasant weekend?"

"Yes, very pleasant. Did you?" she asked calmly.

His teeth flashed in a crooked grin. "Yes, I must confess I did."

This was insane, she thought wildly—they couldn't be talking like this with what was between them. But they were. She listened with professional expertise as he ran down the day's agenda.

At length he closed the folder and folded his hands. Absently, he picked up the tiny carved deer and ran a finger down its satiny flanks, then set it aside for the jet-handled letter opener. As he looked at her again, the evasive quality of his gaze disturbed her more than this uncharacteristic fiddling with objects on his desk. Christina braced herself for whatever was coming. The tension he radiated was very visible to her perceptive eyes.

"Miss Lacey, I won't be needing you for a while. But I don't want to lose your excellent skills entirely. Our chief accountant's secretary has just taken a maternity leave, and I'm sure he'd be delighted if you filled in during her absence. It's noon now, so why don't you report to him after lunch. His name's Paul Kinslow, and every woman on the eleventh floor worships him, so I think you'll enjoy working for him," Daniel said, smiling.

Christina felt her face paling, the sensation of skin drawing so tightly around the planes of her face that she touched her cheek in dazed alarm. She was too stunned to react for an agonizing instant, but from somewhere deep inside she found the resources to tilt her chin and match his pleasant manner.

"Yes, Mr. Belmont. Paul Kinslow, you said?" Something was buzzing in her ears and she shook her head to dislodge it. Seeing his eyes on her face, Christina hastily rubbed her ear. "I spent the week-

121

end sailing—which means that half the time I was upside down in the water and I think I've still got water in my ears. I—well, good-bye, Mr. Belmont," she said insanely.

"Hardly good-bye," Daniel blandly reproved. "You're only going one floor down."

"Yes, I suppose so. Oh, I left the UMC file with Diana. There were some typos—not mine, I assure you," she added with a wintry smile. "And by the way, I want you to be the first to know. I'm going to marry Greg Stafford. Good-bye, Mr. Belmont."

Christina turned sharply and strode from his office. She hadn't the vaguest idea why she had said that—it was an out-and-out lie and *why* had she said it! She didn't even intend to see Greg again.

A car horn shocked her to awareness. She was half a block from the office, crossing the street against the light . . . going to lunch, she recollected. Walking served a better purpose than eating, her brain independently decided.

She had just been ignominiously demoted, Christina supposed, but this was curiously irrelevant. Daniel didn't need her; *that* was the knife that turned again and again. His face had remained indifferent to her momentary betrayal of distress. He didn't need her, when his smile lent purpose to her day. . . .

Shocked to note the time, Christina hurried back, taking the elevator to the accounting department. *Just one floor down, Christina,* her heart mocked.

Paul Kinslow was short, chunky, and endearing with enormous brown eyes blinking behind horn-rimmed glasses and a kinky fuzz of hair circling his bald dome like a halo.

"I'm so glad to see you, Miss Lacey! I've been

snowed under since my secretary left—I can't even find my desk!" he moaned.

There was no help for it, Christina thought with a tiny uplift of spirits, she might just adore this man right along with the rest of the eleventh floor! "I'm very happy to be here, Mr. Kinslow. And finding lost desks just happens to be my specialty," she said warmly.

It was also her salvation. Christina existed in a self-created vacuum that first week, submerging her battered self in the anodyne of work. She did not see Daniel, but she did learn through Paul's tactful comments that Daniel had implied that she had requested the change.

Although this was appreciated, Christina seriously doubted that anyone with a lick of sense would believe she chose a position in Accounting over being Daniel Belmont's personal assistant. Well, *she* certainly couldn't explain it—she wasn't sure herself exactly why she was now Paul Kinslow's secretray. Since it was impossible for her to think ill of the man she loved, she had vaguely resolved the matter in Daniel's favor. What had occurred between them was just as much an embarrassment to him as to her.

Knowing this was merely her own supposition, Christina nevertheless clung to it as desperately needed support. The fact that her privileged parking slot yet bore her name did wonders for morale, and coming to know this sweet, gentle man she now worked for was a peculiar pleasure in itself.

"You're okay," she assured herself when anxiety threatened to overwhelm her. "Just do your job and don't think—you're *okay.*" It proved a workable formula, and she was pleased at how well she functioned under severe stress.

Greg Stafford still pursued her. Neither polite discouragement nor refusals to see him made an impression. Christina was uncertain how to handle him. Except for that one unpleasant incident, he had been kind to her, and she hated the thought of hurting him. Yet she had no desire to resume their relationship. Cursing her cowardice, she caved in to his persistence and agreed to a dinner date, then agonized over what she must say to him.

As it happened, she could have spared herself this torment. When she opened the door to Greg that night, she learned the consequences of her spiteful last words to Daniel. He and Greg had coincidentally lunched at the same restaurant that afternoon and Daniel had apparently offered warm congratulations on their engagement.

Greg's jubilant words were a crushing blow to Christina. Daniel didn't care, had even offered congratulations on her engagement to another man. Numb with shock and a profound sense of betrayal, she accepted it. She was completely unconnected with any of this, standing aside, blankly watching a scene taking place in her apartment. Only when Greg presented her with a ring did she rebel. She didn't want an engagement ring, and she refused to accept it.

She saw him every night that week, not by choice, but by the fervor of his desire, and her stunning inability to function outside the office. Each time Greg embraced her Christina looked at him with complete lack of emotion, although she did marvel now and then that he seemed so unaffected by her remoteness. She ought to feel *something*, she thought. All she felt was frozen.

Paul Kinslow congratulated her and Mrs. Coyle

stopped her in the lobby one morning with a rather puzzled look along with her warm wishes. Christina supposed the entire building knew she was to become Mrs. Greg Stafford, but since it didn't matter to Daniel, it didn't matter to her. She simply did not *care*.

Christina never knew exactly what shattered her deep sense of detachment, but its ending was as stunningly swift as its onset. As she left her office Friday evening, nearly three weeks after being banished from Daniel's, she stepped out into the lovely autumn sunlight and was suddenly, explosively angry. That she had been drifting into a marriage she did not want with a man she did not love struck her as incredible enough, but that she had *allowed* it! My God, what on earth has possessed me! she thought incredulously. Feeling strong and purposeful, she directed her car into traffic, her mouth tightening as she thought of what must be done tonight. The anger surged even more sharply—she should never have permitted things to go this far! But she had, she thought grimly, and now she had to set it right.

When Greg arrived precisely on the stroke of eight, she invited him in and, in a gentle but firm voice, ended their relationship. He took it badly. After he stormed out, she cried awhile, but it seemed to Christina that for the first time in weeks, she had done something that merited praise. At least one area of her life was now cleared of complications, she thought wryly. Daniel Belmont and her love for him were matters beyond her control.

She slept soundly that night and felt so energetic next morning that she cleaned the apartment from top to bottom and still needed something to do. Since she had no suitable fall attire, she decided on a shopping spree, which promptly raised a ticklish question. The accounts opened by Belmont Enterprises were still active, but did she have a right to use them? The clothing allowance was one of the fringe benefits that went along with her job, and Daniel had temporized his decision to let her go with "for a while," which surely meant that she would eventually resume her proper position, and if she was not prepared—Christina laughed aloud as she imagined his splendid wrath.

Having happily solved her clothing dilemma, she headed for the shopping mall and its delectable boutiques.

When she emerged from the mall with her arms full of packages, Christina was surprised by the wintry wind whipping the awnings. During the five hours devoted to shopping, the temperature had dropped nearly thirty degrees; one of Texas's famed blue northers had swept down on the city and November now felt like winter.

She hadn't even bothered looking at coats—who would have thought winter came in the space of a single afternoon! "Back to the arena, Christina," she sighed.

Two hours later, marvelously exhausted and hungry, she again left the mall, her arms laden with shopping bags.

Greg called that night, and again Sunday, but she remained firm. She was no longer a weak, vacillating person, Christina thought with relief. She treated herself to dinner and a movie and fell asleep that night to the sound of a lulling rain.

Monday morning she rushed to the window to

check the weather, hoping this cool snap had held. It had. Her arms were goosebumped by the time she slammed down the window. Moving with youthful vigor, she attended her morning toilet, then delightedly selected a three-piece ensemble consisting of a slender skirt and jacket in wool jersey and a whisper of silk crepe-de-chine blouse. The slim jacket sleeves were cut to display elegant French cuffs, and the voluptuous splash of geranium silk was marvelously effective against the sleek, wheaten suit.

And who was there to see it? Christina lost her grip on the optimistic hope that had been sustaining her. She had always believed in fairy tales when she was a child, but as a woman she should be capable of separating myth from fact. Love stories didn't always end happily. Especially love stories as improbable as the one her romantic mind persisted in writing.

Her elation ebbing, she put on black crocodile pumps and unwrapped a sheer wool cape as soft as velvetized cream lined with pale yellow satin. She fastened the gold buttons with a fleeting smile; at least Mr. Kinslow would appreciate this chic young woman who walked into his office with a cheery greeting.

She was correct. His roguish wolf whistle was so outrageous they were both overcome with laughter. And God, it felt good to laugh about something.

In early afternoon she was taking a break when a deep masculine voice interfered with her breathing. Not daring to turn, she gazed blankly at the opposite wall as Daniel strode into Paul's office and shook hands with the bubbly little man.

"Well, Paul, I need a favor. Knowing Miss Lacey's competence, you're doubtless well caught up by

127

now. I'd like to borrow her for a few days—looks to me like she's none too busy," he said teasingly.

Oh, Daniel! Chiding her hammering heart, Christina slowly turned and let her eyes feast on the face she had so sorely missed.

"Miss Lacey." Daniel inclined his head. Deep green eyes took an instantaneous eternity to complete their appraisal.

Poker faced, Christina copied his gesture and murmured, "Mr. Belmont." Her voice betrayed no hint of the glorious tumult in her heart.

Daniel turned back to Paul, who promptly began praising Miss Lacey to the skies. Daniel cut him short with an indulgent laugh that brought alive the curved lines in his cheeks, and Christina's fingers screamed their aching need to touch!

"I agree she's a marvel," he said, flashing her another grin. "If it won't disrupt you too much, I would like to have her right now . . ." His eyes caught hers and held for an instant before he looked at Paul. "That is, if Paul doesn't object. Is that all right with you, Miss Lacey?"

Was it all right with her? She would only stab darling Paul with his own letter opener if he dared object! "Of course, Mr. Belmont. I am, after all, a loyal employee of Belmont Enterprises, and I go where commanded—from nine to five," she said silkily, marveling at her steady voice when she was mentally turning handsprings around the office. Where was her pride? Smothered under an avalanche of plain and simple joy.

"Very well. We leave at four. Can you be ready to leave for Mexico in an hour?" Daniel asked, quirking an eyebrow.

Mexico? In one *hour?* If that wasn't just like him,

she thought joyously. "Yes, Mr. Belmont," she demurely agreed. Unable to resist it, she flashed, "Do you think I might possibly be allowed to stop off at the ladies' room before the plane takes off?"

Both men burst into laughter. Daniel's eyes warmed her, moving over the upswept hair and splash of silken bow at her throat, down to the slimly rounded hips and thighs, the shapely legs and ankles, all in a twinkling flash of time. "Possibly," he drawled with a lazy smile that did impossible things to her heart.

Paul kissed her cheek. Handing Daniel her cape, she stood quietly while he draped it around her, his knuckles grazing the back of her neck. When she looked up at him, his face was a smiling mask closed to her scrutiny. She fervently hoped her expression was similarly guarded. Could he hear her heart pounding, this singing in her soul? She loved him. It said everything.

It was damp and cold when they emerged from the building. "I'll pick you up at your apartment in forty minutes," Daniel said. She nodded. "Maybe you could tell me where you live," he remarked as she started for her car. Flushing radiantly, she told him, and scurried for shelter. She refused to question this glorious reprieve. It was enough just to feel this deliciously happy!

Chapter Eight

When she began packing, Christina remembered he had said nothing about how long they'd be gone, so she had no idea of what to pack. Mexico would be warm, wouldn't it? Imagine, *Mexico!* She had never been there. And to go with Daniel . . . Feeling in danger of floating out the window, Christina grabbed ahold of her fizzy self and tugged down the entire set of luggage.

By the time she filled it, Daniel was rapping at her door. "Are you ready, Miss Lacey?" he inquired as he strolled into the room.

How long had it been since anyone had called her Miss Lacey like that! "Yes, sir, I'm ready," Christina said. It was impossible to contain her joyous smile, but Daniel was not looking at her. He swore softly as his eyes wandered over the little room before making contact with hers again.

"Why the hell do you live in a place like this?" he asked roughly. "Surely the salary I pay you is more than adequate for decent living quarters?"

Christina's cheeks grew hot as she saw the room through his eyes. All her brightening little efforts looked more pathetic than colorful. "Yes, more than adequate. But my mother's illness was very costly. The bills outran her insurance, so I . . . well, they're my responsibility, you see," she said evenly.

"I see. Well, let's see if we can get all this down to the car. Good grief, what have you got in here?" Daniel groaned as he picked up the two large valises.

"Well, you didn't tell me how long we'd be staying," Christina indignantly pointed out.

"Humph. Are you sure the kitchen still has a sink?" he growled.

"Yes it does! Would it be too much to ask how long we'll be staying? And exactly where in Mexico are we going?"

"Would it be too much for you to get the door? And we're going to Cozumel and we're staying at the Hotel El Presidente. Now wait here until I manage to get these to the car, then I'll return for the rest."

"But where's Cozumel?" she asked, darting around him as he made his way to the door.

"An island off the Yucatán Peninsula. Didn't you take geography in school?"

As Christina stared at the sleek dark head disappearing around the corner, she was seized with a ridiculous urge to laugh like an idiot and an equally strong urge to hurl her purse at him. Since she could do neither, she sat down on the couch and muttered a few choice words.

Within minutes after they boarded, the silver and

131

blue plane rose into the air and broke through the gray cloud mass into sparkling sunshine, and Christina sighed with delight. She settled deeper into the velvety gray seat and covertly watched Daniel, smiling as he brought out the thermos and coffee cups and opened his briefcase.

"Does something amuse you, Miss Lacey?" Daniel inquired, looking up in time to catch her broad smile.

Nothing could deflate her spirits, not even that stern face. "No, Mr. Belmont."

He grunted. Christina's smile grew embarrassingly wide. He had changed his formal black suit for a blue blazer and slacks and dispensed with a tie. As he studied a long sheet of figures, he raked a hand through his hair, hopelessly tousling the glossy cap.

"Miss Lacey, why am I being smiled at?" he asked without looking up.

"Well, isn't that better than being stabbed?" she asked liltingly. He grunted again, but she saw his mouth twitch.

"My coffee, Miss Lacey?" he resignedly prompted —and she burst out laughing. Of little things like this is love created, she thought. Daniel shook his head with a baffled look, but his mouth was having a difficult time of it. As she filled their cups, he briefed her on the following day's agenda; a long, tedious meeting that would include lunch and, that night, a formal ball in his honor at the home of the eminently wealthy Don Ramon Villines.

"Is he really a don?" Christina excitedly asked.

Daniel grinned. "No, it's pretentious nonsense," he confided. "But it pleases him and it's to my benefit to please the gentleman . . . and so will you,

Miss Lacey. He has a liking for tiny, flower-eyed women." Christina's swift breath raised his eyebrows in mock chagrin. "Miss Lacey, I assure you I do have limits to what I'll do to satisfy a client."

"Huh . . . I'm not so sure of that," she muttered.

Daniel seemed unable to decide whether to laugh or chastise. He gave it up and returned to his work. Christina did not mind being ignored. She was used to it, and besides, she thought happily, it was enough to sit here with him in their private world high above the clouds and just watch his beautiful face.

Where was her pride? she wondered again. When she located the tiny, insignificant lump, she flinched at its smallness, but Daniel looked up just then and murmured, "My coffee?" with such vast resignation to his fate, she delightedly laughed again.

Flinging down his pen, he sat back and regarded her merry face. "Try not to be so grim, Miss Lacey," he admonished. "The meeting tomorrow is the only business on our agenda. There'll be time to enjoy Cozumel, I promise. I was told it's a beautiful place," he soothed.

"I'll try to cheer up," Christina said bravely. She unfastened her seat belt and tucked her feet beneath her, squirming around until she found a comfortable position. Daniel watched her with a curiously hungry smile. She glanced at him, then *looked* at him, and said the first thing that popped up from her tender heart.

"Have you been taking proper care of yourself, Mr. Belmont?"

Daniel looked startled at the gentle query. A brief smile touched his mouth. "It's been difficult, but I daresay I've managed," he dryly returned.

Color tinged her cheeks. "I only meant . . . well, you look rather tired, that's all," she said defensively.

A lovely mist of sunshine on clouds blanketed the land below. Daniel regarded it for a time before resuming the conversation. "I guess I am tired. Maybe I need a vacation. I haven't had one since I took over Belmont Costruction."

"Not one?" Christina asked, incredulous.

"I told you once, eighteen hours a day, fifty-two weeks a year . . ." he shrugged. "Actually, the reason I look tired is, I had a little too much to drink the night before last and spent all day yesterday trying to find my head," he confided.

Christina looked terribly disapproving. He laughed. "Not what you think, Miss Lacey. I was celebrating an anniversary—a toast, of sorts, to a great lady."

"I see," she said, studying her hands.

"I doubt you see," he mocked gently. "I was drinking to the tenth anniversary of Belmont Enterprises . . . and to the woman who started it."

"The *woman* who started it?" she echoed in astonishment.

"Um-hm," he murmured.

She waited. He studied the clouds some more. "If you stop there, I shall—well, I don't know what, but it'll be something drastic," she warned.

"I don't doubt that," Daniel said so dryly she put her feet on the floor and set erect in a most menacing fashion.

His eyes twinkling, he held up a pacifying hand. "All right, all right, if you'd just pour my coffee—"

"I'll pour no more coffee until you've satisfied my curiosity," she declared. "A woman started Belmont

Enterprises? I thought you did—created it with your own two hands, you said."

"So I did. But I had to have a push . . ." The sooty lashes fanned down to shield his eyes. "There was a woman once, a someone I cared enough about to hurt like hell when she found a someone with considerably better prospects than the heir to a two-bit construction firm . . ." He glanced at her. "No need to look so tragic, Miss Lacey. It was the best thing that ever happened to me."

A sardonic smile twisted his lips. "It was powerful incentive to become something other than the owner of a two-bit construction firm. So I gave the lady her due and drank a toast to her mercenary little soul, wherever it may be. Had a hell of a hangover, though," he ended in an accusing mutter.

Christina was torn between laughter and tears. His cynical dismissal of love betrayed didn't fool her for a minute, she thought fiercely. How old had he been when it happened—twenty-one, twenty-two? Young and proud and in love. And then . . .

She wanted to weep; she wanted to ask a thousand questions and comfort the answers. But Daniel's face was getting that closed look again, as though they had overstepped a boundary and he was annoyed at having been so careless.

Delving into his briefcase, he withdrew a sheaf of papers and frowned at her. "Well, let's get to work. Is there the slimmest chance of getting another cup of coffee before we arrive in Cozumel?" he asked sourly.

She had been on the verge of reaching out to him. Jolted into awareness of who he was and who *she* was, Christina uncapped the thermos and assumed a diffident manner. Her heart was soaring higher than

135

the airplane. Just to be here, under any condition, was a sweet foretaste of heaven, she thought softly. Tipping her head back against the seat, she lowered her lashes and hungrily watched him until Daniel handed her a file and suggested she familiarize herself with its contents.

Their hands touched in the transaction. Thrilled by the brief contact, Christina lowered her flushed face and began to read. In what seemed an incredibly short time the plane began its descent.

After the wintry gloom of Corpus, Cozumel was a glorious surprise. The breeze caressing Christina's face blew straight off a luscious tropical isle, and she inhaled the blend of exotic scents. Dusk had fallen by the time they left the airport in the most hilarious excuse for a taxi she had ever seen. The wind mercilessly whipped her hair, but the rear windows weren't rolling up this evening, the driver charmingly explained. Christina was enchanted.

Hotel El Presidente was guarded by enormous sentinel palms and tall torches flaming in the wind. The latter struck her as symbolic of the way she felt—like a fragile flame.

This was, according to Daniel, one of the most luxurious hotels on the island. Christina was unaccustomed to so much naked concrete, and she felt faintly disappointed as she followed Daniel and the dark-faced little man along the exterior stone corridors. However, her room was large and airy and swept by a deliciously cooling sea breeze.

"Oh, this is lovely," she said to Daniel. "Come look!"

Obligingly, Daniel sauntered over to the window where she stood gazing at a pewter sea in the last of the sunset. Christina shivered as a cool, lazy wind tugged at her face, while his body heat spread like caressing fingers down the entire length of her back. "Isn't it lovely?" she repeated.

"Yes, Miss Lacey, very lovely," Daniel said softly. He stepped closer behind her, and the tension in him radiated over her skin in blithe disregard for clothing. For a taut instant his tight-muscled thighs brushed her rounded bottom in a sensuous, breathtaking caress. Unintentional, she soon realized. Daniel stepped away from her with alacrity.

"Ten minutes to freshen up, then we'll have a bite to eat," he said as he walked out the door.

Her three-piece suit was much too warm for this climate. Christina changed to a dressy black-and-white geometric print, low necked and sleeveless, exchanged her pumps for high-heeled sandals, and brushed out her hair. By the time she had dabbed perfume in strategic spots, he was knocking at her door with his usual impatience.

His greeting was laconic, and he overlooked her change of attire. They dined in the attractive dining room overlooking the pool; lusciously ripe mangoes sliced in sweet cream, fresh spinach salads, thick steaks with fried plantains, and a marvelous tray of cheeses took precedence over their conversation.

After the silent meal, Daniel escorted her back to her room. "How's Stafford these days?" he asked, too casually.

"Fine," she said shortly. Daniel nodded and left her with a pleasant good night.

Christina started to change to a swimsuit, but thought better of it. Although it was barely nine o'clock, she was surprisingly tired. Slipping on the barest excuse for a nightgown, she got into bed and read for a few minutes, then yawningly snapped off

137

the light. Sleep came easily as she listened to the murmur of the sea.

She was up with the sun come morning. After a hasty toilet, she dressed in a simple yellow sun dress and sandals and raced from the room. In the light of a golden day, the hotel was vastly more attractive. She walked slowly along the stone corridor, letting her eyes feast on the seascape visible above the waist-high rail. She felt so joyously alive, it was an effort not to skip like a child.

Christina knew it was an irrational joy, but after weeks of just existing, this sun-sparkled morning was sensuous delight. Somewhere in it lay the certain fact of seeing Daniel. That was, to be honest, her only certain fact, yet it seemed to be the reason for drawing her next breath. Cramming down thoughts that would blight her soaring spirits, she sped down the front steps and stopped to look at this thrilling morning.

One decrepit taxi was parked in the circular drive with a fast-asleep driver sprawled in luxurious ease behind the wheel. The hotel rose up in a series of stark exterior corridors, which she now decided were charmingly different. Christina gasped aloud when she spied the monstrous rubber tree growing at the side of a courtyard. Thick, ropy aerial roots dangled from its topmost branches—it was magnificent! Was the tiny three-foot tree that grew in her living room even the same species?

Deep purple bougainvillea roofed the tiny courtyard, and the smell of summer jasmine and honeysuckle teased her senses. Delightedly exploring, Christina started as she spied Daniel lounging against the veranda watching her with a lazily amused smile. If she was a source of amusement, then so be it. She would not bother to conceal her childish enjoyment.

She greeted him gaily, waving an all-inclusive hand as she exulted, "Isn't it *gorgeous*, Mr. Belmont!"

"Yes, lovely," he quietly agreed. Tall and lean in faded blue denims and a clingy knit shirt, he sauntered over to join her with a rueful look that demanded sympathy. "Do you know what I've discovered, Miss Lacey? The dining room doesn't open until seven—I can't even get coffee!"

Christina's mouth curved appropriately downward. "How terrible! But it's six forty-five now. You can surely survive another fifteen minutes without coffee."

The black brows knitted together in a scowl for her pert dismissal. "It's hardly to be taken lightly, Miss Lacey. You know what a bear I am until I have my coffee."

Gravely, she agreed, her heart dancing in thrilling awareness. She did indeed know his predilection to grumpiness in the morning—what a privileged thing to know about Daniel Belmont! Her smile faded. Not such a privilege, she thought, turning away; many other women must know this fact far more intimately than she.

Subdued by the intrusion of reality, she said shortly, "Well, I'm going to explore for another fifteen minutes."

"I might as well join you," Daniel sighed. When she stumbled over a tree root, he looked up and said, "Oh, give me your hand!" She gave it. His slim, tanned fingers wrapped warmly around her small ones, linking them together tightly. It was so nearly a reflexive reaction she inwardly sighed and her heart began its soft love song again. His hair glistened in the sunlight, and his bronzed skin seemed to glow against his white shirt. The thin knit fabric clung to his broad shoulders and massive chest. The power of him, she thought with a quick little shiver that manifested itself through her fingers, the sensuous, thrusting power of him in tight blue jeans.

They circled the back of the hotel, emerging upon a wide stretch of beach that sloped down to an enchanting little cove between sheared coral walls. The beach was artificial, Daniel supplied. "And I'm getting sand in my shoes," he added accusingly.

"So am I!" she laughed. Christina took off her sandals and ran barefoot across the deliciously hot sand. Grabbing the bole of a palm, she swung around it, calling excitedly, "Hurry up! Look at these things—like a cluster of enormous grapes. Are they coconuts?"

"Yeah, green coconuts," he said sourly.

"Oh! Can we pick one?"

"I don't believe one picks a coconut like one picks a grape. In any event, they're about three feet above our heads—and I am not about to climb a tree, Miss Lacey!"

"Grouch," she said mischievously.

After breakfast and several cups of what he declared to be absolutely inexcusable coffee, Daniel stood up with a brisk, "Time to work, Miss Lacey."

Christina gazed out the window to a bed of ferns and greenery. She wouldn't have been at all surprised to see a unicorn among the ferns, while he saw nothing but commonplace plants.

Much of her ebullience dimmed as they walked to their rooms to dress for the meeting with his Spanish clients. She might as well face the facts, Christina fumed, half running beside the tall, coolly detached man already absorbed in his thoughts. Despite the lovely surroundings so hauntingly conducive to romance, it was business as usual.

Appraising eyes met hers as he paused at her door. "Something quiet, simple, attractive," he said, his gaze flickering down the bright yellow sun dress and flowing black hair.

"I know how to dress by now!" she snapped.

"Sorry. Force of habit, I guess," Daniel sighed. "Oh, by the way, I'd advise sticking to the Perrier water we had at breakfast."

"Yes, I will. Mr. Belmont, you never did tell me how long we're staying here," she reminded on a quieter note.

Daniel swung around. "I haven't decided yet. Why? Have you some reason to hurry back to Corpus?" he asked sharply.

Surprised, Christina shook her head, setting her hair to swaying about her shoulders. "No. I was just asking, that's all."

Narrowed green eyes bored into hers from a cold, set face. "Are you quite certain, Miss Lacey? After this meeting I·won't be needing your professional services. If you want to return, just say the word and I'll have you on the evening flight to Texas."

Christina stared at the hard, almost belligerent set of jaw. His chin was out-thrust, his face very near hers. Bewildered at his sudden anger, she freed her wrist from the hand that unthinkingly gripped it.

"No, of course I don't want to return. I said I was just asking, that's all. When you're ready for me to go, then I'll go. Excuse me, please?" She spared him a thin smile, opened the door, and went inside. What the devil, she wondered, was that all about?

As she changed her clothes, Christina's face screwed up into a puzzled frown. Her perceptions were just as sharp as ever. Leaving aside his momentary anger, Daniel was still a very tense man—much more than this Mexican proposal warranted. Was her presence causing that tension? If so, then why was he so flatly averse to her leaving?

She slipped her silken feet into respectable pumps and sat down to tame her hair. It would be nice if just *once* she had answers to her questions.

Chapter Nine

She seemed to step from sphere to sphere with breathtaking speed, Christina thought. Yesterday she had been in Texas, this morning and most of the afternoon in Cozumel, pretending to be an office machine in one of the most tedious business sessions she had ever endured, and now she was in Mexico City, sitting beside Daniel in a chauffeured limousine, driving down what must surely be one of the most fascinating boulevards in the world.

"Paseo de la Reforma," she said, trying out the name. Daniel indulgently smiled and pronounced and accented the words correctly for her. He had stretched an arm across the back of the seat, and she felt his fingers playing idly in her hair as he pointed out particular sites of interest. Ever sensitive to his slightest touch, she focused her attention out the window. Which was not all that difficult, Christina conceded. The difficult part was keeping her cool.

Daniel laughed and ruffled her hair as she helplessly exclaimed over yet another enchantingly ornate building. He had said nothing about Greg or that other unpleasantness. Christina longed to probe, but she dared not; although once their interminable meeting was concluded he had mellowed into a charmingly relaxed companion, she yet sensed something just below the surface that made her uneasy.

Besides, she stoutly reminded herself, living only for the moment was the one fast rule she had set for herself this fairy tale trip. At least much of his earlier tension had vanished and he seemed to be enjoying playing tour guide. Some tour, she thought wistfully; from airport to hotel—in this case, the Villines's home. She settled back with a very long sigh.

Daniel looked down at her and asked, "What now?"

"I was just thinking of all the lovely cities we've been in, and all I ever see of them is the view from our plane window—or car window or hotel window . . ."

"Unfortunately, that will be the case with this one. We're leaving early in the morning. Maybe someday . . ."

As much as she would like to, Christina did not pursue that intriguing "maybe someday." They were entering the Villines estate, and she sat up with a snap of excitement. Daniel had briefed her a little more on their hosts for this night, and her eagerness had an undercurrent of apprehension. Don Ramon and his wife sounded positively frightening. Daniel said he had not met Sēnora Villines, but she was reputed to be as imposing as a queen, and their home was a showplace in a city that boasted an incredible number of palaces.

The limousine wound through a lovely parklike area and soon drew up before a palatial residence of warm red brick. A servant bowed them inside, where they were shortly joined by a notable gentleman with piercing black eyes and a shock of silver hair.

"Christina Lacey, may I present Don Ramon Villines," Daniel said after their effusive greeting.

Bowing effortlessly from a very trim waist, Señor Villines gallantly kissed her hand. *"Bienvenidos,* Señorita Lacey—*mi casa es su casa,* which means welcome and my house is yours," he said grandly. "Ah, here is my wife."

Christina sincerely hoped she was not gaping, but the woman who walked through the door was the most magnificent creature she had ever seen, strikingly handsome with her wide cheekbones and coronet of black hair. And the enormous diamonds glittering in her ears certainly did nothing to detract from her queenly appearance!

"And my daughter, Isabella Elise," Don Ramon concluded, stretching out an elegantly groomed hand to the tall young woman who had entered the salon from an exterior door.

Christina felt instantly diminished. If her mother was queenly, Isabella was a tawny-skinned Mayan princess. Her dark, sultry eyes immediately lit on Daniel. She flashed him a bewitching smile, her accented voice as seductive as her manner.

Christina was dying to look at Daniel. His husky greeting held an appreciative note that grated on her ears as he gallantly kissed the hand Isabella extend-

ed. After the introductions were completed the
señora deftly herded her guests into a charmingly
informal room that obviously formed the family's
private living quarters. Bidding everyone to sit down
and be comfortable, she clapped her hands, and two
pretty young maids whisked in and out with trays of
drinks and hors d'oeuvres.

Daniel was supremely at ease, but Christina felt
tongue-tied and awkward despite the general air of
cordiality. "Your home is simply magnificent, Señora Villines," she candidly exclaimed. After that,
nothing would do but that Isabella take Miss Lacey
on a tour—something neither Miss Lacey nor Isabella desired, but they obeyed.

Her peripheral brushes with wealth notwithstand-
ing, Christina had never seen anything to equal the
Villines home. Isabella kept up a rapid-fire chatter as
they strolled by masses of exotic flowers in carefully
tended beds and what seemed to be a horde of small,
white-garbed gardeners charging about.

Isabella's question came softly. "You are Señor
Belmont's secretary, are you not? And you are here
in that capacity?"

"I am Señor Belmont's secretary, and I am here in
that capacity," Christina agreed evenly. Studying
that enchanting smile, she saw clearly how it would
be tonight. Isabella would be on Daniel's arm, and
she would be the odd woman out. How could she
have thought it would be any other way?

Graciously declining the young woman's offer to
show her the miniature lake, Christina set off for the
house with icy dignity. Isabella's red mouth curved
in a satisfied smile that did not go unnoticed.

Daniel and the elder Villines were in one of the
lovely courtyards, sitting in rattan chairs with drinks

and easy conversation. After a proper interval, Christina started to excuse herself with a headache.

"Because of the party, we are dining informally tonight. Would you like to take dinner in your room?" the señora inquired.

Christina gratefully accepted. She was escorted to a sumptuously appointed bedroom. After a long bath, she put on a red velour robe and carried three evening gowns to the bed to make a selection. Christina sank down beside them and rubbed her temples. What did it matter which she chose? Beside Isabella's exotic beauty, any woman would pale to insignificance, she thought, achingly jealous. First the shimmering Lisa and then that topaz-eyed brunette, and now Isabella—why did all Daniel's women have to be such raving beauties!

Christina gave her woeful image a sheepish grin. "You're a mess, you know that? He just met the woman two hours ago!" Nonetheless, even a mess knew when to fold her cards. Hearing Daniel's tread in the corridor, she ran to the door and called out to him.

"Mr. Belmont, I would like to be excused from attending this party tonight? Surely my presence is not required," she said stiffly.

Daniel's face darkened. "What do you mean, your presence is not required?" he demanded.

"I meant that you'll have Señorita Villines on your arm—you won't need me hanging on to your other one, will you?" she said icily. "So I'm begging off—"

"The hell you're begging off!" Daniel exploded. "I happen to *want* you on my arm tonight. Damn it, Miss Lacey, I arranged this whole affair just for you!" His eyes blazing, he gave her a black scowl as her mouth dropped open.

147

"You arranged it . . . for *me?*" she echoed.

"Well, let's just say I put a bug in Ramon's ear about how my secretary would enjoy seeing his beautiful home, along with a sumptuous party to be given in my honor," he said with a sudden devilish grin. It vanished in the mask of icy forebearance just an instant later.

"You are attending the party, Miss Lacey, as my . . . companion for the evening. Since I did not know that Ramon had a daughter named Isabella, I can hardly be expected to escort her. Now when you're dressed—and I do hope you'll look equal to the occasion—someone will escort you downstairs to me. Understood, Miss Lacey?"

"Perfectly, Mr. Belmont," she snapped back. Christina shut the door in his face, seething at his insulting instructions. She was to look *equal to the occasion!* "Damn him!" she whispered through a hot rush of tears.

Wiping them, she walked to the bed to study the three gowns again. Daniel had seen two of them, but the third . . . she shook her head. The third gown had been an impulsive whim and one that required a certain flair to wear with success. It was at once ingenue and wanton, an outrageously romantic dress in white lace and chiffon. Right now she felt about as worthy of it as the proverbial sow's ear, she thought acidly. She regretted having snapped at Daniel, but what had he gotten so mad about?

Señora Villines knocked, then entered the room with a diminutive, moon-faced woman trailing along in her majestic wake. "This is Juanita. She will help you dress, and she is an excellent hair stylist. . . . Problems?" she asked brightly. Within seconds she had disposed of Christina's dilemma. The white gown, of course. "Of course you can carry it off. You are small and petite, but you have style, my dear—never delude yourself into thinking you do not."

Soft dark eyes rested on Christina's face. "And Señor Belmont would certainly choose the white one, because that is how he sees you."

Christina's eyes widened, but the señora was already making her way to the door. Pausing, she fired another staccato volley of words at the maid and favored Christina with a reassuring smile. "I will return for you, and we shall descend the stairs together, yes?"

Confusedly, Christina nodded. She felt ten years old going on a hundred.

As soon as her mistress closed the door, Juanita swung into action. The white gown was carefully donned, fastened, zipped, and white satin slippers practically bowed onto her feet. Deft hands coiled her hair in a graceful pouf of curls lifted high off her neck and fastened with a single white orchid. Juanita carefully arranged tiny curls at the nape of her neck, then motioned Christina to stand up. Feeling deliciously pampered, she readily obeyed.

"¡Que bonita!" the maid exclaimed as Christina slowly turned before the mirror. The slender skirt fell from a brief lace bodice, clinging to her hips and outlining the tantalizing hint of her thighs in a cloudlike drift of fabric. The scalloped lace neckline setting just off her pretty shoulders called for jewelry, but she had nothing suitable.

Or so she thought. The señora knocked and swept through the door with a velvet jewelry box. "Ah, yes, just as I suspected," she murmured, opening the box to remove a sparkling bit of necklace. "I thought perhaps you might lack suitable jewelry for such an enchanting gown. It calls for the tiniest bit of color," she said as she fastened the necklace around Christina's neck. The exquisitely fine chain looked incapable of supporting the single drop of green fire suspended just above her breasts.

"Oh, señora, it's beautiful," Christina breathed.

"And quite appropriate," the señora agreed.

"May I ask, why are you being so kind to me?" Christina softly asked.

"Spanish women are hopelessly susceptible to small, apprehensive creatures," the woman laughed. "I am not putting you down, you understand. It's just that I too have known the breathless anxiety of ten million butterflies assaulting my stomach."

"You?" Christina said, doubting.

"Yes. I was not always as you see me now . . ." Chattering lightly, the handsome, serenely composed woman maneuvered Christina down the grandeur of marble stairs.

The ballroom was dazzling with a thousand twinkling lights. Christina's pulse throbbed in her throat as a familiar dark head turned slowly in her direction. Emerald eyes deepened to bottomless pools. Caught in glory, Christina waited.

"Miss Lacey." The shining head inclined as he offered a white-clad arm.

"Mr. Belmont." She tipped her chin, taking it. Her eyes danced over the handsome face attempting to retain its hauteur. "Mr. Belmont? This is all a little . . . scary," she confessed.

"Nonsense," he said crisply. And it was.

Isabella was stunning in Venetian blue silk. A new glint touched the long black eyes flowing over her gown as Isabella noted both Christina's stunning change of appearance and the hand resting firmly

under her elbow. Daniel guided her to an appreciative Ramon, and eventually she was introduced to
the other guests, a bewildering assortment of Spanish men and their regal ladies.

"Where did you get that necklace?" Daniel asked
keenly, leaning to her ear.

"Señora Villines loaned it to me."

"It's very lovely," he idly remarked, moving
her on.

At length, he held out his hand and asked, "Shall
we, Miss Lacey?" and took her off to the dance
floor.

The wickedly stirring music set up a throbbing in
her blood. Flushed and laughing, she stumbled
through the dance in a futile, merry effort to follow
his agile feet through intricate steps.

"Oh, all right, I give up!" she exclaimed, throwing
up her hands in appealing surrender to her inept-
ness. A round of warm laughter applauded her
impetuous outburst. Christina blushed as she met
Daniel's mischievous eyes.

"Why, Miss Lacey, this is a first. You, surrender?
Concede a victory?" he whispered, pretending to be
terribly shocked. Comporting herself with dignity,
she released his hand and glided back to the table,
flinging a provocative little glance over her shoulder.

"Please honor me, Señorita Lacey?" Don Ramon
promptly requested.

"But I was terrible at that," she protested.

"Ah, but that is because you did not have a good
teacher," he said, flashing Daniel a rakish grin. And
he was absolutely right, she told Daniel later—she
had not had a good teacher; Don Ramon made it
simplicity itself to follow his steps.

"Perhaps that is because the teacher did not

distract you, Señorita Lacey," Daniel whispered as he gathered her into his arms for another dance, mercifully slower this time. He held her lightly and at a correct distance, but she was so alive to his touch, he might as well have been embracing her. Wondering if he too felt this shivery attraction, she brushed her fingertips across the back of his neck, and the muscles in his arms tightened in instant response. Delighted, she looked up at him through the veil of her lashes.

"Do that again, Miss Lacey, and I can't be held responsible for the consequences."

The low, husky warning was a tingling thrill. He laughed softly at the color rising from her creamy throat to tint her cheeks. Caught in shyness, she lowered her eyes and finished the dance in silence.

Daniel danced often, displaying a dashing style new to Christina. While it was pleasing to observe him with the señora and other matrons, it was exceedingly painful to watch him take the beautiful Isabella in his arms, to note her possessive hand on his sleeve as she captured him for introductions to her friends. Her manner was finely circumspect, but there was no mistaking the fact that she found Daniel Belmont a highly desirable man.

Well, what woman wouldn't? Christina reflected. He was easily the most attractive man there. Isabella would be less than a woman if she did not respond to that magnetic masculinity.

It was all very well telling herself this, but it did very little to alleviate the sharp stabbing pain of jealousy. Covering the slender, bejeweled hand on his arm with his own, Daniel joined a circle on the other side of the room and Christina felt painfully the sense of having been carelessly forgotten. Jeal-

ousy, she knew, was an acute form of insecurity—
but when had she ever been secure with Daniel?

She was given no time to brood. One keen glance
from the señora and Don Ramon was at her side
inveigling her into another challenging dance. Afterward, Christina accepted another glass of cham-
pagne and thirstily sipped it. Miserably aware that
Daniel and Isabella had sat down at a table to enjoy
a private chat, she fiercely willed herself not to cry.

When she chanced another glance, they were
strolling to the dance floor for another one of those
exciting, whirling dances. Isabella moved with the
lissome grace of a gazelle, her black eyes glittering
like the diamonds she wore. Daniel's long fingers
spanned her waist. His gaze was on her curving
mouth, red and wetly shining as she laughed up at
him, and they whirled around the floor, easily moving through the complicated steps.

Christina was forced to watch, for it was a beautiful performance. Admiring comments and proudly
knowing looks came the señora's way. Everyone
knew the handsome *americano* and the wellborn
Isabella were superbly matched. And Daniel was far
from immune to Isabella's sultry femininity, Christina wretchedly admitted. His lean body snapped with
excitement, the gleam in his eyes subtle male acknowledgment of a beautiful female's charms.

Christina watched them finish the dance to a
round of applause. From then on her expression was
cool and indifferent whenever Daniel glanced her
way.

It was after midnight when he finally chose her for
one of the soulful *corridos,* a hauntingly sensuous
folk song that offered a breathing spell now and
then. Confessing a need for fresh air, he smoothly

maneuvered her out into the perfumed night. A tormented Christina was in his arms, her lips hungrily seeking his, the moment they gained the privacy of the shadowed terrace.

If he was surprised at her boldness, he gave no sign of it. Holding her crushingly tight, his mouth as eager and hungry as hers, they stood enrapt in a spell compounded by the huge white moon hanging above dimly glimpsed mountains. Even while Christina scorned her eagerness, she pressed close enough to feel every line of the exciting body she ached to know more intimately. She was scaldingly aware he would have no difficulty achieving his desires this night. Yet she held nothing back from him. Her tongue engaged his in a breathtaking duel, her hands greedily caressing his powerful shoulders and neck. Flinging caution to the winds, she let all her needy love flow into their long, urgent kisses.

Daniel drew back and dropped his arms lightly around her waist. "We had best return to the ball, Miss Lacey . . . before I compromise your valuable reputation."

His voice held a note of what she assumed to be mocking amusement. Christina went hot with humiliation, but his soft kiss on her lips was dismayingly successful in erasing even this small jot of pride. She dropped her head to his chest and he held her a moment longer, then withdrew his arms from her, leaving her chilled by the absence.

The sweet flame of excitement dimming, Christina gazed across the moonlit gardens. "Why do you think it's so absurd that I value my reputation? It's just possible that the man I marry will respect me for guarding it," she said, very low.

"It's possible he will," Daniel said coldly. "At any rate, we'd best go back in, don't you agree?"

Wishing she could see what expression those green eyes held, she suppressed her hurt, her reply carefully noncommittal.

The ball was breaking up when they eased back into the room. Looking up in time to catch Elena Villines's indulgent smile, Christina flushed hotly. The woman's romantic notions about her two young guests were so far off the mark it was pathetic, Christina thought, forcing her chin to a proud point.

She escaped to her bed as soon as possible, then lay awake with her questions. Why had Daniel brought her here? Why had he even decided he had need of her again, for that matter? It was imperative she fathom his motives, and yet she could not. She felt like a child playing with matches.

These past two days had been a wild seesaw of emotions; one minute she was floating and the next she was brought to earth with a solid bump. Hope, frail and battered, fought to survive against the stark fact that it was highly possible Daniel had merely picked up his secretary again like a discarded toy. Or, even more likely, he had decided to resume the amusing game of seduction simply because she remained a challenge to his prowess.

With thoughts like these, she found the ground jarringly hard when she hit it. He had been so attractive tonight, that vibrant maleness never so magnetic and compelling as when he had whirled her around the ballroom floor. Her love for this baffling green-eyed man threatened to overwhelm her as Christina recollected the blissful moment on the terrace. Perhaps it had had a fortunate ending, she thought sadly. She had been very close to making a fool of herself. Daniel Belmont could not commit himself to a woman. Why should he? He had everything he could ever want.

From the floor below she heard his husky laugh mingling with Isabella's gay, excited voice. Picturing them relaxing in the warm intimacy that comes after a successful party, Christina sighed and stretched between the cool sheets. She had overheard Daniel tell Don Ramon that they would be returning to Texas Friday morning. She had two more days with him, and then what?

The moon had gone behind a cloud and her room was plunged into darkness. Whatever lay behind that tormenting "then what" was just as deeply shadowed and obscure.

Chapter Ten

Christina was roused from sleep at daybreak next morning. Fuzzily wondering what this was all about, she dressed while a maid packed her belongings. When she joined the breakfast table set up on a flower-bedecked terrace, Daniel's indulgent smiled reaped a stony glare. Obviously he had slept very well indeed.

Idly she sat nibbling on a sweet roll and let the conversation resume without her participation. The wind that feathered her hair carried the scent of orange blossoms, and birds floated in a powder blue sky. The vast expanse of lawn was as smooth as a carpet, deep green velvet under the trees. The color of his eyes, she thought, glancing at Daniel. He wore dark gray slacks and a red and white striped polo shirt—and a widening smile as the terrace door slid open.

Her heart sank as Isabella emerged in a lace-

157

trimmed garment reminiscent of an old-fashioned morning gown. Her hair flowed to her hips like a dark waterfall, and her velvety greeting was accompanied by an enchanting smile. Christina could not blame Daniel for his charming attentions. But she could resent them, and feel blessedly relieved when he brought their meal to an end.

They moved en masse to the car purring in the drive. Smiling warmly, Señora Villines took Christina's hands. *"Vaya con Dios,* Christina," she said softly. "Go with God."

"You will bring her back again, ay, Daniel?" Don Ramon added.

"We'll see," Daniel temporized.

Discomfited by the question, Christina said a quick good-bye to Isabella and got into the car. The trip to the airport was accomplished in silence. On board the plane, Daniel tilted his seat to sleep and advised her to do the same.

Christina cuddled up in her seat and studied him from under her lashes. He looked so boyishly appealing when he slept, her heart twisted with longing. How pleasing it would be to kiss that softly relaxed mouth, the long lashes shadowing his cheeks . . . Her eyes grew too heavy for even this bittersweet pleasure. In a very short time they were both asleep.

"Time to wake up, Miss Lacey," Daniel was saying only seconds later.

Rubbing her eyes, Christina grumbled. "I'm *sleepy,* blast it—why did we have to get up at dawn, anyway!"

Daniel laughed and helped her to her feet. "Because otherwise we'd miss the boat."

Christina stopped dead. "Boat?"

"Um-hm. We're taking an excursion down the coast—that is, if we ever get moving!" he groaned.

Christina began moving and asking questions, all of which were answered with an exasperated, "No questions, Miss Lacey. This is a surprise, damn it—one doesn't question surprises!"

"Well, I do."

"Oh, hush," Daniel said. When they arrived at the hotel, he bade her get her swimming things and meet him in the lobby in ten minutes flat. Jeering at her capricious swings of mood, Christina hastened to obey. How could she discipline her galloping happiness? The day was obviously going to be excruciatingly pleasurable. She gave a philosophical shrug. "Live for the moment, Christina," she sighed. It sufficed. For the moment, at any rate.

Daniel was pacing the floor, casting anxious glances down the corridor, when she came running back to him. He grabbed her hand, and despite her protests, she was practically towed out the door and down the oyster-shell path.

The big white boat was already filling when, breathless and laughing, they reached the hotel dock. Christina was enchanted all over again. Other than her sailing misadventures, this was her first time on a boat, and she immediately secured a position at the rail.

They followed the shoreline, which gradually changed from scrub and coral to deserted beaches framed by a backdrop of wind-twisted trees. The explosion of dazzling white sunlight dancing upon gold sands and blue-green water, the foaming wake a fluorescence of miniature rainbows, and a sky an unreal blue were all indescribably lovely. The wind beat at her face and whipped her hair, and she laughed aloud her delight.

Daniel stood behind her, his arms forming a cradle for her body as he gripped the rail. Christina leaned back into him—just a little, just enough to feel his warmth as a caress upon her supersensitive skin. He chuckled as she excitedly pointed out a school of dolphins keeping pace with the boat, then turning in perfect concert and going on their gamboling way.

Christina felt as excited as she looked. All she had seen of Cozumel thus far was the short trip from airport to hotel, and at long last, she thought joyfully, she was getting to do some sightseeing—and with the man she loved! Feeling in danger of floating right out of the boat, she kept a hand on the rail as they strolled the wide deck. Daniel was relaxed, smiling, marvelously personable in his white terry shirt and dark blue trunks. An eyebrow arching, he cast an eye on her one-piece swimsuit.

"Miss Lacey, you're a little out of style," he observed, pointedly eyeing several well-filled bikinis. Christina's blush only widened his grin, but his teasing was too wonderful to resent.

Inspired to her own, she imitated his tilt of eyebrow and eyed the straw hat he wore. "Where on earth did you get that ridiculous hat?"

"Ridiculous?"

"Ridiculous."

"I bought it from a vendor just before we left the hotel. I suspect you're just jealous because I didn't buy you one," he said loftily, snapping the brim.

"Huh," she sniffed. She shot another look at the outlandish hat. "Well, why *didn't* you get me one?"

160

she asked so plaintively, he laughed, sweetly vindicated.

"These happen to be for handsome *caballeros* only, Miss Lacey. However, if you're very good, I might let you wear it," he said after a judicious pause.

"Conceited, arrogant, *and* stingy," she informed the sky, and, God, this was wonderful!

The boat docked before a long expanse of natural beach. They disembarked and headed for a grove of trees that sheltered a rude camp of sorts. Open fires burned between huge chunks of coral, and the tantalizing aroma of roasting meat whetted their appetites. Christina sat down on one of the rough wooden benches and watched as their lunch was prepared by the staff from the boat.

Coolers were opened and soft drinks and Mexican beer were passed among the thirsty guests. There was fish and mounds of broiled shrimp, and quarters of what Christina took to be beef were taken from their spits and brought to the table along with huge pots of spicy black beans and saffron rice. There were long, thin loaves of a most delectable bread and baskets of *platanos,* the fried plantains she had grown to love. Sautéed in olive oil and seasoned with garlic salt, they were much like thick, crunchy potato chips.

The raw conches gathered en route were chopped and added to a mélange of fresh vegetables and native spices, which Daniel pronounced delicious.

"I'll stick to the meat, thank you! It's delicious. I wonder what it is? It has a certain flavor . . . marvelous, but different," she mused, reaching for her third slice.

Daniel lazily grinned. "I imagine it's *cabrito.*"

"Oh. What's *cabrito?*"

"Goat." He laughed uproariously at her expression.

"Well, it—it's quite good, but I think I'll try some shrimp now. These are your normal, everyday shrimp?" she asked suspiciously.

Daniel forked a heap of delectable pink shrimp onto her plate. "Your normal, everyday shrimp, just as this is your normal everyday goat," he blandly assured.

It was an idyllic day. The air smelled of sea and kelp, far back in the grove, as they wandered through twisting secretive paths, it took on a lemony, woodsy flavor spiced with sunlight and shadows. They found nothing of interest here, just the oddly shaped trees and shrubs—nothing save magic, Christina thought as he laughed down at her. Daniel stood naked from the waist up, his lean, smooth-muscled torso glistening like polished bronze in the sunshine. The soft dark hair furring his chest tapered down to a thin, finger-teasing line and disappeared into the waistband of the snug-fitting trunks.

The same dark, masculine hair etched his powerful legs, and the musky, sun-warmed smell of him was sweet, sensuous torment. They swam in warm blue waters and hunted shells on the beach with notable lack of success. Lighthearted and playful, his eyes dancing with devilry, Daniel picked her up and carried her into the water at the slightest provocation. The excitement of naked skin on naked skin glowed in his eyes and hazed hers with desire.

They had both dropped their guard, and they might have been young lovers, she thought achingly, watching the relaxed face shaded by that ridiculous straw hat. What would it be like to have him like this forever, to have those green-green eyes warming every pore, every muscle of her quickening body! Thrill after thrill raced up her spine, yet she tried to convince her foolish heart that this was far too remote. But he was looking at her so warmly, she felt bathed in green fire.

"Let's see if we can walk off a bit more of that feast, hm?" he suggested, and she bounced to her feet. As they strolled down the length of the beach, she unthinkingly took his hand and swung it between them. In this soft blue and gold solitude, seen through the transforming veil of love, everything had a startling clarity. The tangle of sea grapes and ground-hugging morning glories were exquisitely fashioned to the smallest detail of leaf and fruit and flaring lavender flowers; the minute scraps of iridescent shells crushed into a handful of sand were centuries of time dribbling through her fingers. Awed by the ephemeral quality of their time together, Christina floated along beside him in a dream world of her own.

Logic tried to declare that this was only a rather common beach shimmering under the same sun that beat down on Texas. But her heart refused logic. *This* was reality, this crystalline pleasure. She linked her fingers with his and moved closer until their shoulders rubbed with each step.

I love you, Daniel, she thought fiercely, but she murmured, "It's inordinately beautiful, isn't it, Mr. Belmont?"

"Yes, very beautiful. . . . Well, I see they're boarding the boat. Since it's a long way home, I guess we'd better join them, hm?" he said in a low voice.

As they joined the overly festive throng of fellow

163

passengers, Daniel began to withdraw into himself. Christina collected her bag and handed him his hat with a pert quip, but his smile was scant acknowledgment. On the trip back to the hotel he sat down in a chair and propped his feet on the rail to stare broodingly out across the featureless waters.

Christina was bewildered by this abrupt change of mood. She fell into desultory conversation with a honeymooning couple and listened with abstract attention while she searched for a clue to Daniel's behavior. Everyone around them was laughing and talking in lavish enjoyment; the sun was setting the sea on fire, and he sat there looking bored to death. With her? It was possible. They'd spent the last two days practically in each other's pockets, and what signified bliss to her might be wearying him. She threaded her way to the rail and stayed there for the remainder of the trip.

As soon as the boat docked, Daniel reappeared at her side and helped her down the gangplank. His introspective silence held until they reached the door of her room. Moody green eyes regarded her sun-flushed face. "Did you enjoy the day, Miss Lacey?"

No use lying, Christina thought. "It was the loveliest day of my life. Thank you . . . Daniel," she said softly.

"I'm very glad you enjoyed it. Well, let's try to get some of this sand off our skins, hm?" he returned with a sardonic smile, and strode on down the hall.

Not quite certain what came next, Christina leisurely bathed and dressed in a flirty little sun dress and high-heeled sandals, then went down to the lobby, wondering if they were to dine together. As she stepped past the stone grillwork that enclosed a small interior courtyard, she heard his familiar laugh. Daniel was having a drink with a woman Christina remembered seeing on the boat, a willowy redhead with a stunning figure and eyes that held knowledge far beyond Christina's.

Her heart began to pound with slow, sickening beats as Christina watched them together. The woman leaned her face to Daniel's to speak in low, intimate tones, and his response was a delighted laugh, a gay click of glasses, and amusement sparkling his eyes as they drank to her remark.

"Well, at least he isn't bored now," Christina thought bitterly. Taking a final look at his animated face, she returned to her room.

When she had shut the door solidly behind her, Christina crossed the sunlit room to stare at her own white-faced image. Curious that it was so white when she was livid with hurt and jealousy. Her hands clenched with self-loathing. "Stupid, idiot, senseless little *fool!*" she spat at her reflection. "What do you have to do, see it in writing? Daniel Belmont enjoys your company now and then, he would like to have you warm his bed now and then, he appreciates your professional skills, and that is *it!* You're no different from any of the other women he uses to amuse himself, no different—"

Christina began to laugh as she heard her ragged voice. It was funny in a twisted, black-humored sort of way. Here they were on this lovely, made-for-romance island, utterly alone to all intents and purposes—and Daniel was downstairs with his redhead and Christina was up here carrying on like a Shakespearean tragedy *and it was just too funny!*

Bitterness had a strangely metallic flavor, she discovered. Deciding she had best do something physical before she exploded, Christina changed her dress for a bikini and went down to the cove to take out her frustrations on the water. After a vigorous swim that rewarded her with muscle fatigue if nothing else, she left the cove and wandered down the rough, coral-strewn path.

A chunk of coral made a satisfyingly uncomfortable perch on which to sit and think as the seductively soft dusk gave way to a brilliantly clear night. The vast black vault of sky was sown with an infinity of stars, and the moon spun a path of beaten silver across the perpetually moving waters. She felt small and lonely and a little frightened in this skin-prickling solitude. But somehow it all served to emphasize the fact that she was an ordinary woman with a very ordinary problem.

She gazed out to sea and thought about that, her mind cool and analytical. Solutions came easily and without tears, and decisions once made were firmly set. Since the source of her unhappiness was Daniel Belmont and her job, she would dispense with both—a clean severance of all the ties that bound her. To go on like this was only asking for trouble. Sooner or later she would wind up in his bed, begging for his love and demeaning her own.

Christina picked up her towel and began making her careful way back to the cove. She felt much better, quite calm, and drained of the raw inner turbulence that had driven her here. Maybe when she returned to Ohio, all this would fade to the substance of a sweet, misty dream. And maybe, just maybe, she wistfully reflected, given the healing qualities of time and distance, she would even stop loving Daniel Belmont.

* * *

Daniel discovered her sitting under a palm on the beach next morning, enjoying her fresh orange juice and the radiant new day. He sat down beside her with a flicker of uncertainty in his eyes. Christina looked at him as if he was a stranger, a tall, intensely attractive man, but a stanger nonetheless. She would not lay her heart at his feet again. Protecting this vulnerable organ assumed topmost priority.

"Hi," she said shyly, as she would do with any stranger.

"Good morning, Miss Lacey. Where were you last night?"

Sensing the tightly coiled tension within him, Christina kept her voice matter of fact. "I swam awhile, then I followed the shoreline for a while, then I swam some more."

"You walked alone? After dark? That was rather careless, wasn't it?" he snapped.

"Perhaps, but it's my business, isn't it?" she said lightly.

"It's your business unless you go getting yourself assaulted, at which time it becomes *my* business, wouldn't you agree?"

"I don't quite see your point," she said coolly, flushing at the sarcastic reply. "I wasn't aware that you're responsible for my well-being."

"Have you had breakfast?" he asked, ignoring her icy tone and abruptly shifting to politeness. His negligent gaze noted the brief bikini she wore, the waterfall of curls tumbling down the back of her head.

"Yes. I was up early this morning, had a swim, then breakfast. Have you?"

"No." He studied the far-off whitecaps frosting

the iridescent waves. As green as his eyes, Christina thought, watching him from behind shielding sunglasses. Presently he too donned a pair, and she felt deeply saddened at the forbidding countenance he presented.

Since he was again remote and withdrawn, she did not attempt conversation. A hardening of her tender heart had been the result of last night's activity before she returned to her room. Let him do as he liked, she was through with Daniel Belmont. When she returned to Corpus, she was leaving the lovely city where love had flowered and wilted without anyone taking notice.

Her decision had left her curiously at peace. Or maybe just numb, she mused. Whatever—it didn't matter. They were leaving Cozumel in the morning, and there remained just the rest of this day to get through. She permitted herself a lingering look at the long, tanned legs and slender feet. As powerful and disturbing as the rest of him, she thought. His hair was tousled by the brisk sea breeze and curled enchanting over his brow. Restraining her urge to touch it, she got up and left him sitting on the beach.

The need to avoid him was acute, but there was simply nowhere to go, Christina thought despairingly. The hotel was splendidly isolated and to leave it one had to take a taxi—to where? She supposed she could ride into town and amble around by herself, but the idea was singularly unappealing. Hounded by a vague, restless anxiety, she prowled through the hotel grounds until she encountered the young couple she had met on the boat. Learning they were going skin diving on the other side of the island, Christina asked if she could tag along.

"Of course," the pretty young bride agreed. "Do

you have diving gear? These are the clearest waters in the world, and there are some gorgeous reefs out there. This is our third time out!" she enthused.

Wishing she hadn't been so distracted when they exchanged names on the boat, Christina replied, "No, I don't have gear. I just wanted to explore. Actually, all I want to do is just get out of this hotel," she added candidly.

"Yes, it is rather confining, isn't it? Well, get your things and come along with us," the woman replied.

What was her name, Christina thought. Jean? Joan! "Thank you, Joan—won't be a minute," she said. Dodging a tall, green-eyed man making his way rather grimly through the lobby, she sped to her room and grabbed up some beach gear.

A few minutes later, they were barreling down the road in their rented Jeep. The other side of the island was austerely beautiful, with sheltered coves lying between monolithic blocks of coral, over which waves showered spray many feet into the air; it was a wild and picturesque area devoid of habitation.

Once they arrived at the designated spot, they arranged a meeting time, and Christina set off for some solitary exploring. If only Daniel were sharing this with her! Recalling the look of boredom on his face, she angrily shook off the wistful thought. She could enjoy this just as much alone, Christina told herself. She decided to climb the coral despite the alarming fact that its surface presented a hazard of dagger points and rough little pits just deep enough to entrap a foot. It was like presenting a small boy with a challenging tree, she conceded, preparing to tackle it.

Reaching the flattened top, Christina stood erect and looked around her. There was the ocean, furiously slamming waves at the coral, the sky pouring down into it, merging with and becoming one on the distant horizon; just to her left, sea water geysered through a blowhole and drenched her with a spray, catching rainbows and destroying them in the space of a breath. All very pretty, she fully confessed, but now she had to get herself back down this treacherous coral.

When she descended with nothing more than a scratch on one ankle, Christina splashed through the clear, shallow water and sat down under an eroded coral arch. She had lost all interest in exploring. It was no fun alone, and she might as well admit it. Her little spit of dry land was cool and shadowed, and she felt tired, hungry, and very much like crying. She spread her towel and lay down for a much needed nap.

It was long after three when her new friends awakened her. They shared lunch sitting under the shaded arch, the newlyweds' happiness splashing over Christina like sparkling water. A suggestion to explore the town gained her enthusiastic support. The longer she could avoid Daniel, the better, thought Christina.

She found the native market small and rather disappointing and jammed with tourists from the sleek white luxury liner anchored just offshore. The main attraction was relatively inexpensive jewelry fashioned from black coral dredged up from the ocean around Cozumel. Really quite pretty, Christina thought. She splurged on a necklace and, impulsively, cuff links for Daniel, then irritably wondered why. She would never have the courage to give them to him.

After investigating every colorful stall, they had a

drink at an outdoor café sheltered from the sun by a solid roof of wisteria vines. Crickets hopped about their feet and music wailed so loudly they had to shout their comments to one another. It was mass confusion and should have been utterly delightful but her heart felt like it was bleeding.

"I can't begin to tell you what this day has meant to me," Christina said. Excusing herself, she returned to the market to buy something special for two warm, wonderful people who had willingly shared their happiness with a stranger. Finally she purchased a coarse-textured serape woven in gay colors.

As Christina walked back to the café, Daniel's gift burned through her skirt pocket. She took a firmer grip on the bulky serape. At least this was one present she would have the courage to give.

Chapter Eleven

The sun was setting by the time they returned to the hotel. Tossing her parcels on the bed, Christina bathed, then donned a long, silky beach shift. She felt strangely listless, as if something had broken inside her and thrown her usually graceful movements out of kilter. The finality of *tomorrow* was a knot of tears clogging her throat.

Setting the hairbrush on the dresser, she shook out her hair, and adjusted the saronglike garment. It was definitely not her usual mode of dress, but it satisfied an inner recklessness. The ankle-length skirt sported side slits reaching to her thighs, clinging snugly to her hips and winding up and over her bosom to tie carelessly about her neck. Wondering if Daniel would approve of it, she smoothed the supple fabric. She had bought it at the native market and it would probably fall apart at the first washing, but it was fetchingly pretty right now. Its glowing pinks and reds against her sun-kissed skin, her high cheek-bones combined with the cloud of satiny black hair flowing around her shoulders, gave her an exotic look, and the effect, she was pleased to note, was devastating.

The perfume she misted about her was rather unnecessary. She frowned as she applied more to her wrists. Why all this care with her appearance—a last-ditch effort? A discomfiting thought. Refusing to even consider its merits, she thrust it aside and left the room. Just this evening to get through, she told herself, then it was good-bye island and good-bye Daniel Belmont! Oh, *damn*, why did it have to hurt so much!

The balmy air and last golden light of sundown mocked her heartache as Christina walked out of the hotel. In the pretty little cove swimmers frolicked in shimmering green water and voices and laughter hummed around her on waves of pleasing sound. Out on the raft that marked the boundary of the swimming area, two sea nymphs spread themselves to the sky, one of them, Christina noted with a catch of breath, the lovely auburn-haired woman she had seen with Daniel last night.

Which immediately brought up the question of Daniel's whereabouts. Christina scanned the area, but there was no sign of him. Deciding she might as well sample one of those exotic-looking half-coconuts filled with rum and pineapple juice, she wandered over to the small thatched bar near the pool and gave her order. Sitting nearby were her friends the newlyweds. They invited her to join them, but Christina refused. They were warm and kind and she liked them very much, but there was such a thing as being a nuisance. After all, they were on their honeymoon. And too, she thought wryly, turning back to the bar, she could not stand being splashed with any more of someone else's happiness this day.

She jumped at Daniel's voice behind her. "Easy on the rum," he arrogantly instructed the bartender.

Christina turned and looked at him, tall and powerful, so powerful. Did he have any idea what just the sound of his voice did to her? Green eyes, framed by long, silky lashes and darkened with some inner turbulence, gazed steadily at her face. She felt so vulnerable and insecure, irresistibly drawn into the depths of those beautiful eyes! Shaking her head to break the spell he so easily wove around her senses, she turned from Daniel. Her love for him was as much a part of Christina Lacey as breathing, and she knew with a deep, inner certainty that it would always be so. Last night's brave assumptions were only wishful thinking, she bleakly confessed. Time and distance would not dim the bittersweet torment of loving Daniel Belmont.

A stolen glance at him confirmed what her heart knew with a vengeance. He was clad in fitted brown slacks and a soft saffron shirt. The warm rich color was striking against his tanned skin, the deep V of the neckline revealing the masculine hair that swept up to the base of his throat. As he scrawled his signature across the bar tab, his lean, hawkish profile was mellowed by the lock of hair dipping over one eyebrow—her special weakness, Christina achingly admitted. She masked her longing with an eloquent shrug.

"I do thank you for your concern, Mr. Belmont. I had no idea these drinks were too strong for me," she said sarcastically. Picking up her diluted drink, she walked off. To her surprise, it was deliciously refreshing. She might, she decided, have a dozen of the things.

Daniel fell into step beside her. "Did you enjoy your afternoon?"

"Lovely!" she sang out. A wildfire of rebellion was building inside her, burning off apathy like sunshine on a spring morning. She put a provocative swing into her steps and felt every quiver of it.

"I'm delighted," he stated. His tone changed to one of utmost casualness as he inquired, "By the way, have you and Stafford set a wedding date? I've received no invitation, and I thought surely I'd be invited."

Startled into stopping, Christina stared at him. "Oh, don't be absurd," she snapped.

"I wasn't aware that I was being absurd—it sounded a logical question," he said evenly.

He meant it, Christina thought with astonishment. It had not occurred to her that Daniel might still think her engaged. She went breathless for an instant—until she realized it would have made no difference.

"Yes, I suppose it is. I'm not marrying Greg Stafford. I told him from the first that I didn't love him and had no intention of becoming his wife. I also told him good-bye last week," she said colorlessly.

Her flat response had a stunning effect upon Daniel. The shining green gaze burned into hers, and whatever emotion he was feeling tightened the angular planes of his face to stark prominence. How was she to interpret the sudden bleakness washing into his eyes?

175

Daniel stepped back from her, his voice peculiarly thin and strained. "And you didn't think this worth mentioning to me?"

Christina shrugged. "I saw no reason to, no. What concern is it of yours?" she coolly returned, walking on.

Daniel caught her arm. "Look, I—I thought we'd have dinner in town tonight, maybe some dancing afterward?"

The odd uncertainty in his manner weakened hers. Only her mulish pride prevented her from reaching out with forgiveness. Was she such a fool then? Christina bitterly jeered her tremulous longing. But was this any better—to be left achingly lonely and bereft, needing and never having? Oh, of course she could *have* him—he was only too willing to share with her the side of Daniel Belmont other women enjoyed. Her will strengthened as she remembered last night's agony. Perhaps she could live with knowing he didn't love her, but she could never endure the torment of knowing she had to share him. And she would *not* be influenced by these confusing new tactics he'd thrown into the game!

Icily she lied, "I already have a dinner date. Sorry."

His hands shot out and gripped her shoulders. "Then I suggest you break it!" Daniel flared.

"Is that a suggestion, Mr. Belmont? It sounded more like an order."

Daniel released her and raked a hand through his hair. "All right, it's an order," he growled. But it was a soft growl, husky with undisguised emotion.

"May I remind you it's after five?"

A trace of his old arrogance struck his clefted

176

chin. "I'm well aware of the time, Miss Lacey. Now sit down."

Christina's mouth tightened as she met him look for look. "Oh, okay," she said, yielding. "I suppose, since it's the last order you'll be giving me, I can obey with grace." She settled on the lounger, careless of the enticing slit of skirt, and crossed her ankles with languid ease. Her skin looked dusted with gold, she thought, running a caressing hand down one shapely leg.

"The last order?" Daniel repeated, settling in a chair beside her. Despite his fluidly relaxed body, he had an explosive air about him.

Christina took a deep breath. She might as well get this over with. "Yes. Tomorrow morning, when we return to Corpus, I'm going back to the office only long enough to say farewell to Mr. Kinslow, then I'm returning to Ohio. I'm through with Belmont Enterprises," she said. There was no insolence in her voice, merely quiet determination.

"Don't be absurd, Miss Lacey. You know I couldn't possibly get along without you," he reproved.

"Yes, you can. You've already proven that. You got along without me fine for three weeks, didn't you?" she reminded.

"Those were the most miserable three weeks of my entire life," he said quietly.

Deriding the thump of her heart, Christina kept her voice inflectionless. "They were? Why was that, I wonder?"

"Um. I suppose I became accustomed to having an assistant," he said.

"Oh. Well, you can find another one easily enough," she remarked.

177

"I'm sure I can." Daniel leaned his head back against the bright orange cushion and closed his eyes. Christina indulged herself in a caressing look down his slim, virile body, then studiously examined the scratch on her ankle. At a weary sigh from Daniel she asked, "Tired, Mr. Belmont?"

"As a matter of fact, I am. I didn't get much sleep last night." He sighed again.

"Well, she was very pretty," Christina silkily agreed.

Daniel's eyes flew open. "What the hell are you talking about?"

"Oh, come now, Mr. Belmont, such modesty doesn't become you. I came down to the lobby last night to see if we were dining together and I saw your redhead," she acidly returned.

Daniel's baffled look changed to amusement and relief. "So *that's* why . . . Miss Lacey, you have an annoying habit of jumping to conclusions. Last night I sat down to have a drink and the young lady walked over and asked if she could join me. Naturally, being a courteous man, I said yes. I finished my drink and went looking for you to see if *you* would join *me* for dinner!" he said furiously.

"Well, I can hardly be blamed for thinking the obvious," Christina defended herself. "After all, she was beautiful, and that's your only requirement!"

"Now where on earth did you get such a stupid idea?" Daniel mused. His devilish grin flamed through Christina, knocking awry all her firm resolutions. "I also happen to have a terrible weakness for fetching, flower-eyed girls in red sarongs," he happily confided.

Christina shot him a furious look. "You're playing with me!"

"I would like to, Miss Lacey, but you won't let me," Daniel reminded, openly laughing.

Oh, God, she hated him! Christina lunged off the chaise lounge so fast that drops of the rum drink spattered her dress. Brushing wildly, she looked at the laughing man, thrilling to the grace of his languid body even while her voice rose in outrage.

"You insensitve . . . *beast!*" she choked.

"Ah! Something original for a change," he said, looking highly pleased. When she wheeled and started up the beach, he called warningly, "Come back here, Miss Lacey!"

"If I wasn't a lady, Mr. Belmont, you would—oh!" Christina gasped as she collided with a chubby gentleman. "Oh, I'm *sorry*—did I splash you?"

He laughed, brushing rum off his atrocious shirt. "A little, but it washes."

"I apologize again," she said. Tossing her coconut into a trash can, Christina turned back to her green-eyed tormenter, her demeanor changing on the instant. "And *you*—" she began menacingly, hands on hips and violet eyes flashing.

"Miss Lacey, spare me the hissing kitten bit?" Daniel implored. "Now let's go have dinner in town—I've heard of a restaurant which not only features absolutely delicious *cabrito,* but sea turtle as well. You may wear what you have on. I rather like that dress . . . those slits . . . most intriguing," he mused.

"Mr. Belmont, I am one step short of physical assault," Christina warned through her teeth. He looked so delighted, she wanted to fling herself against that broad chest and kiss the mouth curving with a joyous laugh. She glared ferociously at this self-betrayal, and at him. To her utter astonishment,

Daniel scooped her up and spun her around, clasped tightly to his chest as he threw back his head in a literal explosion of laughter.

"Miss Lacey—my enchanting Miss Lacey! How could I have lived all these years without you?" he exulted. Christina's stupefied face was drenched with blazing little kisses that covered every square inch of skin and then some.

"M—Mr. Belmont, put me down—let me go!" she cried, pushing at his shoulders. The world had gone crazy and she dared not take an incautious step!

"My sweet Miss Lacey, I'll never let you go!" Daniel joyously proclaimed. "Don't you know that by now? Don't you know why the last three weeks were so miserable? My love, I missed you so! I found myself saying your name, I found myself hurling empty coffee cups at innocent furniture, I found myself pacing the floor at four in the morning . . . I found myself totally incapable of living through another day without you in it."

Her eyes enormous with disbelief, Christina stared speechlessly, wondering if she could possibly have heard the words she had, incredibly enough, just heard. The look in his shining green eyes filled her veins with a wine so intoxicating she sagged in his arms.

"You missed me?" The words were barely audible.

"Miss Lacey, I love you," Daniel huskily replied.

"But—but I don't understand," she said in genuine bewilderment.

"Oh, God. No, of course you don't. Only you are indescribably, unforgettably lovely. Capable of stopping my heart, of making me forget every vow I made—capable of driving me insane with jealousy when I saw another man holding you in his arms."

"I swear, there was nothing—Greg never—" she stammered beseechingly. She could not form a coherent thought over the tumultuous joy flooding her entire being.

Daniel cradled her face in his hands and kissed her, then withdrew with another unbearably tender smile. "Sweetheart, I know that. After I'd cooled off a bit, I realized my exquisite Miss Lacey would not possibly permit such a thing." An eyebrow quirked. "After all, hadn't she withstood *my* advances for months, hm?"

"You're impossible!" Christina joyously informed him.

The eyebrow winged higher. *"I'm* impossible? You drove me crazy, Miss Lacey—crazy enough to come all this way for a meeting that could have been held in my office, crazy enough to actively consider ways in which to dispose of Greg Stafford without leaving clues, crazy enough to connive and inveigle a friend to throw a wildly romantic party that might possibly influence you to—"

Christina's lips stopped his words. Hungrily he gathered her into his arms. She cuddled deeper with a happy little sigh. "Oh, Mr. Belmont," she murmured with such content he laughed.

"Oh, Miss Lacey," he mimicked, kissing her again. And again.

Christina held him tightly, feeling his heart beating under her cheek, his virile strength thrillingly evident in the arms around her. "My darling, I love you—with all my heart I love you," he whispered. Would she ever tire of hearing that! Rapturously she gazed into the handsome face aglow with love—for *her,* she thought incredulously, for Christina Lacey. She was gloriously proud . . . and it was too wonderful to be true.

"Why did you send me away, Daniel?" she asked guardedly.

"Because I had to put some space between us just so I could think clearly," he said slowly. "Sweetheart, I'm sorry if that hurt you—and I know it did. I saw your face when I . . . Christina, listen and try to understand? What I told you on the plane, about the woman responsible for starting Belmont Enterprises —darling, I made a joke of it, but it was no joke—I thought I had the world by the tail, baby. I had just received my engineering degree and become an active partner with Dad, I was young and idealistic and in love . . ."

He sighed deeply. "Maybe it was love, maybe it was just badly mauled pride, I don't know. But whatever it was, it was damned painful, and I swore to myself I'd never let a woman get that close to me again." The last of the sunset splashed into the sea. Daniel drew her very close and laid his cheek on hers.

"Everything just seemed to go to hell then. Dad died just a month later, and I was so filled with hurt and bitterness, sometimes I thought I couldn't hold it all! But I had a refuge—the company he'd left me. I threw everything I had inside me into creating Belmont Enterprises. When I finally stopped to take stock of myself, I found I was past thirty and cared deeply for no one or nothing, except my creation. . . . Lonely, sometimes, but I was also fairly wealthy and secure of myself, in sole command of Daniel Belmont. I was satisfied with what I had achieved, perfectly content . . . or so I thought."

Daniel looked into eyes as soft and tender as a fawn's. "And then one evening I was sitting in a hospital room at the bedside of a woman I had inadvertently put in that bed and suddenly these enchanting eyes were looking at me out of the most woeful little face I'd ever seen, and this thin tiny voice said—accusingly, of course—*it hurts*. And from that point my life turned upside down," he ended indignantly.

"It's hardly something to laugh about, Miss Lacey," he reproved her. "I was no longer in control of myself. Half the time that self didn't even know what the hell it was doing! All I did know was that it was unthinkable—positively, aggravatingly *unthinkable* that Miss Lacey would not always be within touching distance. Sometimes I caught myself feeling so idiotically happy I had to snap at you to regain my balance," he said with a rueful grin.

He kissed her. "I didn't like what was happening to me, damn it! After all, I had run Belmont Enterprises alone for ten years. Why did I now feel it would be impossible to continue without Miss Lacey by my side?"

"Because you loved me," Christina tremulously affirmed. It still seemed improbable, and she had a desperate need for reassurance.

"Well, yes, but I didn't know that," Daniel aggrievedly replied. "That time you quit, just walked off and *left* me, I went a little demented. I tore that damned town apart looking for you! Possessed with only one thought—to make certain I would walk into my office the next morning and find you there." His voice deepened. "Waiting for me, looking so lovely and sweet the sun began shining at the precise instant you said, 'Good morning, Mr. Belmont!' *That* was your job, Miss Lacey, darling—making the sun shine for me."

"Speaking of my job, do I go on with it—as your assistant, I mean?" she asked breathlessly.

"Um, that's up to you, baby. But it would be wonderful to leave everything just as it is, and certainly stimulating to know that the lovely little secretary sitting there demurely taking notes was coming to me that night, to my arms, my bed . . ." His kiss roughened in passionate endorsement of his words.

Christina turned to ice in his arms. She was still reeling with the abrupt transition from dreams to reality, and she put the blackest possible interpretation on his words. *Everything left just as it is—in his arms, his bed.* Not a wife, but a mistress. That was all he wanted! Why had she assumed a declaration of love was automatically followed by marriage?

Because you're a sentimental, starry-eyed little fool, of course, she scathed her foolish heart. Let Daniel utter a few love words and you're off and running, spinning fantasies with wild abandon! She was drowning in a sea of pain, a dark, seething tide that would surely bear her away!

"Oh, darling, I want you," Daniel whispered, his words a concise summary of her bitter thoughts. Christina lowered her head to repress the tears gouging her eyelids.

"I'm sorry, Daniel," she said tonelessly, "I don't want to continue as your—your assistant or anything else." Her icy control snapped under the crushing weight of disillusion. "I have no desire to share your bed or see to your damned sunshine. Let me *go!*" Seeking the shield of darkness but too distraught to think, Christina wrenched free of his embrace and ran toward the lighted pool area.

"Christina? Christina, wait!" Daniel's astounded voice failed to stop her, but his hand succeeded quite well. Jerking her to a screeching halt, he asked furiously, "What the hell's the *matter* with you?"

"Mr. Belmont, why don't you take a dive into that pool?" Christina hotly invited. "Or the ocean. Take your pick, but do it!" She loathed that baffled face, she thought in chaotic fury.

"Damn it, Miss Lacey, no wife of mine tells me to go jump in the ocean in front of half the whole damn world!" Daniel thundered.

"I am not your . . . *wife?!*" Her voice cracked as his words fully penetrated her hazed brain.

"No, but you're going to be—and I will not have my wife telling me to go jump in the lake!" Daniel delivered in an awesome roar. Glancing at their vastly interested audience, he raked his hands through his hair as he looked at the dumbstruck woman frozen in her tracks. *"Damn!"* he muttered incredulously.

"We're getting married?" Christina breathed.

"Yes, we're getting married. Miss Lacey, you are the most maddening, infuriating, aggravating woman I have ever met! You're a hindrance to my work, a detriment to my peace of mind—you are driving me insane, Miss Lacey! I love you, do you understand? We are getting married, do you understand? *Do you understand, Miss Lacey?*" he ended on a baffled roar of pure masculine outrage.

"You're telling me? Not asking me?" Christina joyously scowled.

"Yes, I'm telling you!" Daniel looked at her, at their audience, back at the flushed, defiant face he adored. "No, I'm not telling. I'm asking, Christina. Will you marry me?"

"Oh, Mr. Belmont!" Christina hurled herself at him with such force, Daniel stumbled backward as she landed on his chest.

"It would be damned good to hear you say it," he gruffly commanded.

"Yes! Yes, I'll marry you!"

"And?" he prompted, a pleading note stealing into his voice despite his stern look.

"And I love you—I've always loved you—that's why I hated you so, you impossible, insufferable, tyrannical man!" Christina lovingly assured.

Minutes later, Daniel became aware that they were kissing for an audience who had risen as one and were delightedly applauding the performance.

"Do you think we could take this somewhere a little more private?" he growled.

"Yes, darling," she cooed, kissing him again.

"Miss Lacey." Daniel sighed deeply. The pert face and shining violet eyes gazing adoringly into his reaped another one. "Let's get out of here," he suggested huskily. Holding her firmly in his clasp, Daniel propelled them from the pool area, across the sand and to the far edges of the beach. "Come here, Miss Lacey," he whispered.

"Yes, sir. Daniel, are you going to call me Miss Lacey all the rest of my life?" she asked curiously.

"As much as I love the name, I suppose I shall have to call you something more fitting, like Mrs. Belmont." He sighed as she nibbled about his neck. "Christina, I've heard that people can be married very quickly in Mexico. I don't know *how* quick, but perhaps if I called Don Ramon and request his assistance . . . Would you be satisfied with a very short engagement—like one night?"

Christina nibbled his ear. "I begrudge even one night, my darling."

"I promise you the honeymoon we'll have will more than make up for it," Daniel groaningly assured. "Come here, love, come here . . ."

His arms tightened until she was wrapped so snugly against him they were one silhouette in the moonlight. Hungrily he sought her mouth, the virile sensuality of him becoming a wild pagan delight coursing through her blood. Christina let go of the last tiny shred of doubt and yielded to the unfettered joy of her beloved's passion, her lips warm with honeyed urgency.

It was the essence of lovemaking in a kiss, the sweet, fiery promise of the ecstasy to come, the total absence of doubt and the rapture of complete trust. It was love, Christina thought with what small facility she had left for thinking, the stuff of moon-spinning dreams . . .

The intrusion of voices very nearby finally caught their attention. "This is not such a private place, Daniel," she sighed.

Daniel laughed, low and husky, his eyes shining in the moonlight. "Miss Lacey, I have a whole room full of privacy," he whispered on her lips.

Genuine Silhouette sterling silver bookmark for only $15.95!

What a beautiful way to hold your place in your current romance! This genuine sterling silver bookmark, with the distinctive Silhouette symbol in elegant black, measures 1½″ long and 1″ wide. It makes a beautiful gift for yourself, and for every romantic you know! And, at only $15.95 each, including all postage and handling charges, you'll want to order several now, while supplies last.

Send your name and address with check or money order for $15.95 per bookmark ordered to

Simon & Schuster Enterprises
120 Brighton Rd., P.O. Box 5020
Clifton, N.J. 07012
Attn: Bookmark

Bookmarks can be ordered pre-paid only. No charges will be accepted. Please allow 4-6 weeks for delivery.

N.Y. State Residents
Please Add Sales Tax

Silhouette Romance

IT'S YOUR OWN SPECIAL TIME

Contemporary romances for today's women.
Each month, six very special love stories will be yours
from SILHOUETTE. Look for them wherever books are sold
or order now from the coupon below.

$1.50 each

Hampson	☐ 1 ☐ 4 ☐ 16 ☐ 27 ☐ 28 ☐ 52 ☐ 94	Browning	☐ 12 ☐ 38 ☐ 53 ☐ 73 ☐ 93
Stanford	☐ 6 ☐ 25 ☐ 35 ☐ 46 ☐ 58 ☐ 88	Michaels	☐ 15 ☐ 32 ☐ 61 ☐ 87
Hastings	☐ 13 ☐ 26	John	☐ 17 ☐ 34 ☐ 57 ☐ 85
Vitek	☐ 33 ☐ 47 ☐ 84	Beckman	☐ 8 ☐ 37 ☐ 54 ☐ 96
Wildman	☐ 29 ☐ 48	Wisdom	☐ 49 ☐ 95
		Halston	☐ 62 ☐ 83

☐ 5 Goforth	☐ 22 Stephens	☐ 50 Scott	☐ 81 Roberts
☐ 7 Lewis	☐ 23 Edwards	☐ 55 Ladame	☐ 82 Dailey
☐ 9 Wilson	☐ 24 Healy	☐ 56 Trent	☐ 86 Adams
☐ 10 Caine	☐ 30 Dixon	☐ 59 Vernon	☐ 89 James
☐ 11 Vernon	☐ 31 Halldorson	☐ 60 Hill	☐ 90 Major
☐ 14 Oliver	☐ 36 McKay	☐ 63 Brent	☐ 92 McKay
☐ 19 Thornton	☐ 39 Sinclair	☐ 71 Ripy	☐ 97 Clay
☐ 20 Fulford	☐ 43 Robb	☐ 76 Hardy	☐ 98 St. George
☐ 21 Richards	☐ 45 Carroll	☐ 78 Oliver	☐ 99 Camp

$1.75 each

Stanford	☐ 100 ☐ 112 ☐ 131	Browning	☐ 113 ☐ 142 ☐ 164 ☐ 172
Hardy	☐ 101 ☐ 130 ☐ 184	Michaels	☐ 114 ☐ 146
Cork	☐ 103 ☐ 148 ☐ 188	Beckman	☐ 124 ☐ 154 ☐ 179
Vitek	☐ 104 ☐ 139 ☐ 157 ☐ 176	Roberts	☐ 127 ☐ 143 ☐ 163 ☐ 180
Dailey	☐ 106 ☐ 118 ☐ 153 ☐ 177	Trent	☐ 110 ☐ 161
Bright	☐ 107 ☐ 125	Wisdom	☐ 132 ☐ 166
Hampson	☐ 108 ☐ 119 ☐ 128 ☐ 136	Hunter	☐ 137 ☐ 167
	☐ 147 ☐ 151 ☐ 155 ☐ 160	Scott	☐ 117 ☐ 169 ☐ 187
	☐ 178 ☐ 185	Sinclair	☐ 123 ☐ 174

Silhouette Romance

Coming next month from
Silhouette Romances

Dreamtime by Anne Hampson

When Jane left America for the Australian Outback she had high hopes for a happy new life. But there she met domineering Scott Farnham and found herself in a heartbreaking trap.

A Secret Valentine by Dixie Browning

Now that Grace Spencer's life was finally well-ordered and sensible, she didn't need construction worker Quinn Donovan breaking down old walls and building up new expectations in her heart!

Midnight Sun by Mary Carroll

When Tag Hansen's car ran into Lark, she thought it was the end of her holiday . . . until he extended his hospitality and had Lark rearrange all her plans.

Race the Tide by Mia Maxam

Deceiving Scott Kirkner in her mechanics coveralls was fun . . . until Christina fell in love. How could she tell Scott his mechanic was the same beautiful woman he had romanced?

An Adventure In Love by Marilyn Manning

While in London Julie Brewster had agreed to stay with Morgan Stuart, an old friend of her grandfathers'. But Morgan was young and attractive and Julie fell passionately in love!

More Precious Than Pearls
by Susannah Windham

When Manzanillo Arismendi grudgingly offered advertising executive Leeanne Mullins his prestigious account, she knew she could handle it—but handling Manzanillo was altogether another matter.

Silhouette Desire
15-Day Trial Offer
A new romance series
that explores
contemporary relationships
in exciting detail

Six Silhouette Desire romances, free for 15 days!
We'll send you six new Silhouette Desire romances
to look over for 15 days, absolutely free! If you decide
not to keep the books, return them and owe nothing.

Six books a month, free home delivery. If you like
Silhouette Desire romances as much as we think you
will, keep them and return your payment with the
invoice. Then we will send you six new books every
month to preview, just as soon as they are published.
You pay only for the books you decide to keep, and
you never pay postage and handling.